"Are you saying I don't have as much sense as a *horse?*"

Lily demanded, scrambling to her feet. "How dare you! You have the gall to stand there and—"

"We have to go back to the fort." He reached for her arm.

Lily jerked away. "I have no intention of going anywhere with you."

"It's a longer walk back than you think. It'll be dark soon."

She squared her shoulders, a strength she hadn't felt before filling her. "I'll manage, thank you just the same." Lily drew in a great breath. "I'll go back to the fort when I choose. And I'll get there on my own."

"You won't make it," North said, anger creeping into his voice. "Most of the men at the fort will end up out here searching for you, risking their own lives."

And she isn't worth it, his look seemed to say....

* * *

Cheyenne Wife
Harlequin Historical #687—January 2004

CHEYENNE WIFE

JUDITH STACY

HARLEQUIN®

TORONTO • NEW YORK • LONDON
AMSTERDAM • PARIS • SYDNEY • HAMBURG
STOCKHOLM • ATHENS • TOKYO • MILAN • MADRID
PRAGUE • WARSAW • BUDAPEST • AUCKLAND

Special thanks and acknowledgment are given to
Judith Stacy for her contribution
to the COLORADO CONFIDENTIAL series.

ISBN 0-373-29287-2

CHEYENNE WIFE

Copyright © 2004 by Harlequin Books S.A.

Visit us at www.eHarlequin.com

Printed in U.S.A.

Please address questions and book requests to:
Harlequin Reader Service
U.S.: 3010 Walden Ave., P.O. Box 1325, Buffalo, NY 14269
Canadian: P.O. Box 609, Fort Erie, Ont. L2A 5X3

To David, Judy and Stacy—
thanks for keeping me sane.

Acknowledgments

The author wishes to thank the following people for their assistance with this book: Debra Brown, Candace Craven, Martha Cooper, Joan Fry, Jane LaMunyon, Jolene Smith, Bonnie Stone, Tanya Stowe, Gary Kodel, M.D., Greg Holt, National Parks Service.

Chapter One

Santa Fe Trail, 1844

She'd gone to hell.

Lily St. Claire pressed the damp cloth to her brow, desperate for a moment's relief. She'd died. Yes, that must be it, she decided. Because right now, she *had* to be in hell.

The covered wagon lurched, a wheel finding another rut in what some overly optimistic guide—a man whom Lily believed truly deserved to be cast into the pit of eternal hellfire—had referred to as a "trail." She braced her foot against a wooden trunk and grabbed the edge of the narrow bunk to keep from toppling to the floor.

A mournful groan reminded Lily that she was very much alive despite the heat, the suffocating wagon, the foul stench of sickness. The man lying on the damp sheets mumbled incoherently. Sweat trickled from his fevered brow, soaking his hair, his tangled gray beard and his thin white nightshirt.

Her father.

A stranger, really.

For weeks—Lily wasn't sure how many—Augustus St. Claire had burned with fever, flailed his arms, conversed with unseen people, even Lily's mother, dead twelve years now.

Lily dipped the cloth into the bucket of tepid water and laid it on her father's forehead. Fear and guilt crept into her thoughts. Fear that he wasn't getting any better. Guilt that he was dying before her eyes, and she didn't know how to help him.

A wealthy businessman from Saint Louis, Augustus had stunned Lily when he'd told her of his plan to explore the West, to expand his business holdings in the wilds of Santa Fe. His plan to send her away.

Again.

Since her mother's death when she was seven years old, Lily had lived in boarding schools. Fine institutes all, catering to the daughters of the wealthy. She'd just graduated from Saint Louis's most prestigious academy for young women, prepared to do what was expected of her and take her place among polite society, when her father had revealed his intentions.

He'd wanted her to move to her aunt Maribel's home in Richmond, Virginia, where Lily could take up the sort of life she'd been raised to lead. He told her harrowing accounts of Indian raids on the Trail, stories of disease and hardship. Yet for all his attempts to discourage her, Lily insisted that she accompany him. She had to take this chance—perhaps her very last chance—to get to know the man who was her father.

The trip had promised to be an adventure. Before leaving Saint Louis, Lily had been contacted by the editor of the newspaper and was asked to chronicle the trip in a series of articles. She'd packed her journal, her paints and brushes, intending to write poetry and sketch the scenery along the way.

Setting out, she'd envisioned she and her father working side by side to start the new business, carve out a living together in the new land. Finally, they would truly be a family. Lily's heart had soared at the prospect. Perhaps, she'd hoped, he might even tell her all the things she'd longed to hear about her mother.

But barely two weeks into the journey, Augustus had sliced open his leg with a hatchet while attempting to split kindling. A deep, nasty cut; Lily had nearly fainted at the sight.

Her years at boarding school had been spent learning deportment, etiquette, menu planning, the proper way to supervise a household staff. Madame DuBois's lesson plan had contained nothing about medicine.

With no doctor on the wagon train, a few of the older women had told Lily how to care for her father. She'd forced herself to look at the gaping wound, the oozing mustard-colored pus, and endured the stench. She'd sat at his bedside tending to him endlessly. Yet despite everything she'd done, his condition had only worsened.

And grew worse by the hour.

A slice of sunlight cut through the wagon's dim interior, bringing a welcome breath of fresh air with it as Jamie Nelson pulled back the canvas opening. He was only fifteen years old, yet he handled the team of horses like a grown man.

Augustus had hired the Nelsons, a family also heading west, to assist them on the journey. Though they traveled in their own wagon, Mrs. Nelson cooked and cleaned for Lily and her father, while Jamie, their oldest son, took care of the horses and drove the wagon.

Lily's stomach lurched. "Are we there?" she asked, unable to keep the excitement from her voice.

"No, not yet," Jamie said, holding the reins, looking back over his shoulder.

"Is your mother coming?" she asked, her words more a plea than a question.

"Ah…no, Miss Lily," he replied with an apologetic dip of his head.

Why not? she wanted to scream. Why hadn't they

arrived at the fort yet? Why wouldn't Mrs. Nelson walk back to her wagon and help nurse Augustus?

And why wouldn't someone make this nightmare end?

"You—you want to come sit up front for a while, Miss Lily?" Jamie asked. He gulped. "With... me?"

The desire to escape tempted Lily. It wasn't supposed to be like this. She wasn't supposed to be confined in this airless wagon, trying to figure out how to care for her ailing father, worried sick with fear, scared that he might die at any moment.

For an instant, Lily wanted to shout at Jamie to turn the wagon around, take her east again, deliver her to her aunt's home in Virginia. She wanted a bath—a hot bath with lavender scents, a maid to style her hair, fresh clothing. That's where she belonged. That's where Augustus belonged, as well, with real doctors and nurses who knew what they were doing. Neither of them belonged here, suffering under these inhumane conditions, horrified by the constant threat of Indian attacks and fatal disease, filled with an aching loneliness.

Augustus groaned and Lily turned back to him. He mumbled something she couldn't understand. She removed the cloth from his forehead and wrung it in the water, then swiped it over her own forehead, smoothing back an errant strand of her dark hair.

If she weren't here, who would take care of her

father? Again, Lily wondered at his original intention of making this trip alone.

"Miss Lily?" Jamie asked, jarring her thoughts.

She shook her head. "No. No, I'll stay here. With Papa."

"Oh…"

"But you'll let me know when we get there, won't you?" she asked, her excitement building. "When we get close, I mean. When you can see it?"

After the wagon train had reached the Arkansas River, most of the wagons had taken the Cimarron Cutoff, the southern—and more dangerous—branch of the Trail for the final leg into Santa Fe. With her father so ill, Lily had gone with two other wagons along the Mountain Branch toward Bent's Fort. The fort was a center for trade along the Trail, not a military installation. There, they would rest and re-supply before continuing.

"Sure thing, Miss Lily. I'll let you know the minute I see the fort," Jamie promised, then pulled the canvas closed.

Lily gulped hard, forcing back a sudden wave of tears. Once they reached the fort, surely *someone* would make this nightmare end.

"Here comes trouble."

Standing in the shadows of the adobe walls of Bent's Fort, North Walker whispered the words to the horse tethered to the hitching rail. The brown mare rubbed her head against his pale-blue shirt, seeming to nod in agreement, but North didn't notice.

The arrival of covered wagons at the fort—even as few as these three—brought news from the East, a chance to trade goods and services, make money.

But this one had brought something else.

Trouble.

North pulled his black hat lower on his forehead as he watched men step out of the trade room, the kitchen, the dining room. They stood in doorways and lingered in the shadows, staring. North's gut tightened a bit, urging him to cross the dirt plaza as well.

Young white women—especially pretty ones— were rare at the fort and in this part of the country. This one, who had just climbed out of one of the wagons, hardly seemed to realize she was the center of attention as she spoke to Old Man Fredericks.

North kept his distance.

Half Cheyenne, half white, North was accepted by the men at the fort for what he was. A horse trader, a guide, a messenger.

His other activities he kept to himself.

Tall and broad shouldered like his father, North dressed in Western clothing to better blend into the activities at the fort. He had his Cheyenne mother's dark eyes, but his skin was more white than bronze.

His only concession to his Indian heritage was his long black hair, tied at his nape with a leather thong.

His father had been a mountain man who'd left his family and a comfortable life behind and come west with the beaver trade; he'd eventually married a Cheyenne woman. North had learned Eastern customs and Indian ways from each of his parents, and was equally comfortable in the two worlds.

Worlds that were on a collision course.

Evidenced by the young white woman who was still talking to Hiram Fredericks, sending four men scurrying to do her bidding.

Stepping out of a hot wagon after weeks on the trail, she somehow looked refreshed and poised. Dark hair artfully piled atop her head, a dress of delicate, light fabric that flowed in the late-afternoon breeze. There was an economy of movement as she spoke with Fredericks, a grace North had never seen.

A lady.

That's what his father had called women like this one, North realized. Telling his stories of growing up in the East, he'd described the pampered women there, the hours they spent on grooming, attire and appearance, the value they placed on personal conduct. North had thought it outrageous. Hours spent in the practice of walking? Not to surprise an enemy or spring a trap, but to simply look pretty while in motion?

North had hardly believed him.

Until now.

This one moved like the whisper of the wind, a silent call in the wilderness.

Trouble.

North patted the mare's thick neck, content to keep his distance for now.

This woman was trouble, all right.

But maybe just the sort of trouble he was looking for.

Chapter Two

Lily woke with a start and sat up quickly on the narrow cot. A moment passed before she remembered where she was.

The fort, she realized. The room Hiram Fredericks had given her and her father yesterday.

She sank onto the pillow once again.

After the confines of the covered wagon Augustus had crammed full of the goods he intended to sell in Santa Fe, this room seemed like a palatial bedchamber. A solid roof over her head, four sturdy walls, a real floor—even if they were made of the plain adobe of the fort.

Yet any pleasure Lily might find in her new accommodations didn't relieve the anxiousness that hung over her, that had followed her, dogged her since her father had injured himself weeks ago.

She pushed herself up on her elbow, the familiar anxiety that she'd lived with for so long settling upon her like a thick quilt. She eyed her father on the cot across the room, his eyes closed, his breathing even. He slept peacefully, as he had during the night.

A good sign? Surely it was. But, really, she didn't know.

One more thing this journey had shown her she didn't know.

Thank goodness Hiram Fredericks had helped her yesterday. Tall, lean Mr. Fredericks, with his head of white hair and bushy mustache, had proved a godsend. He seemed to be in charge of things here at the fort, though Lily didn't know if he had an official title.

He'd secured quarters for her and her father, arranged for meals to be delivered to their room, and for her clothes to be laundered. He'd had the blacksmith take charge of the horses and their wagon.

Then he'd sent for the fort's medical expert who'd examined her father's wound and changed the bandage; he'd promised to come back twice a day, if that was what Lily wanted. She did.

Lily said a quick prayer of thanks that gentlemen existed, even in this hostile land.

Squinting against the morning sunlight that came in around the shuttered window, Lily washed and dressed. She hadn't left her room since arriving yesterday, but had seen the Nelson family bedding down last night in their covered wagon outside the gate.

How odd it felt to be separated from them, after the close proximity of their wagons on the Trail.

The men in the third wagon who'd accompanied them to the fort had slept outside, also. Lily couldn't remember their names and hadn't especially liked them, anyway, yet she wondered how they were faring.

She would let them know when her father was well enough to resume their travels, and they could all continue on to Santa Fe.

A knock sounded at the door. Lily jumped at the unfamiliar sound. She hesitated answering, still a little uncomfortable in her surroundings, despite the kindness that had been shown her; she wished Mrs. Nelson would come by.

When she finally opened the door, a young man stood before her holding a breakfast tray covered with a white linen cloth. Tall, thin, he had brown hair in need of a trim, and wore clothing that, more than likely, used to belong to someone else; he was no older than she. His generous smile put her at ease.

"Morning, ma'am," he said, and ducked his head. "My name's Jacob. Jacob Tanner. I work over in the kitchen. The cook sent me over here with breakfast for you and your pa."

"Thank you," Lily said, reaching for the tray, genuinely pleased.

"I'd better set it down for you, ma'am. It's kind of heavy," Jacob said, hesitating on the doorstep. "If'n that's all right with you, of course."

While allowing a man into her quarters would be unheard of in other circumstances, Lily decided Jacob seemed harmless—and her life hadn't exactly been filled with her usual circumstances, anyway.

"That's very kind of you," Lily said, stepping back from the door.

"There's broth here for your pa. Cook made it special, just for him." Jacob placed the tray on the little table in the corner, took a quick glance at Augustus in bed, and hurried back outside.

"Did you prepare the other food?" Lily asked, anxious suddenly to have someone to chat with this morning.

"I do some of the cooking, ma'am. But mostly I just fetch and carry for the cook." His cheeks flushed slightly, and his gaze wandered over the door casing before he spoke again. "If you need anything special, just let me know. Mr. Fredericks says we're supposed to take good care of you and your pa."

"Thank you," Lily said. "I appreciate everything that's been done for us. In fact, I thought I'd go over to the kitchen tonight after supper, when the cook's not busy, and thank him personally."

Jacob's expression darkened, and he met her gaze for the first time. He lowered his voice and leaned just a little closer.

"No, ma'am, you ought not be out alone after dark, if you don't mind me saying so," he told her. "It's not safe for a…a woman."

A little chill slid up Lily's spine. "Well, all right. Thank you for bringing breakfast."

"Yes, ma'am," Jacob murmured. He ducked his head and hurried away.

Lily closed the door quickly. Now she really wished Mrs. Nelson would come by.

After Lily ate, she attempted to get her father to drink some broth the cook had sent, but Augustus remained in the deep sleep that had kept him quiet throughout the night and morning.

She was relieved when Oliver Sykes, the man who served as the fort's doctor, came to check on Augustus. He was an older gentleman, not much taller than Lily, who had somehow managed to grow a round, soft belly here in this lean, harsh land.

"He's better, don't you think?" Lily asked, twisting her fingers together as she and Sykes stood beside her father's bed. "He's resting so comfortably now. He didn't wake once during the night."

"Maybe you ought to get some fresh air, Miss St. Claire," Sykes suggested, not looking at her, "while I check over your pa."

A knot of anxiety rose in Lily's chest. "But—but he's doing better, isn't he?" she asked.

Sykes's heavy jowls wobbled as he worried his lips together, his expression growing intense. "You just run on outside for a while."

Lily searched his lined face for a hint of his thoughts, but found nothing.

"Very well," she said, easing toward the door. "But I'll be right outside in case...well, just in case."

When he didn't answer, she slipped from the room and closed the door behind her. She hesitated a few seconds, wanting to go back inside. After all these weeks at her father's side, the separation seemed odd and uncomfortable.

But Mr. Sykes was a capable man—much more knowledgeable than herself. She should leave him to his task, let him handle it. Wasn't that what she'd wanted since her father had injured himself?

Lily turned away and took in the fort. Upon her arrival yesterday, she'd hardly noticed the place in her hurry to get her father settled in a room. Now, she took a good look around.

The two-story fort was the only major permanent settlement on the Santa Fe Trail, according to what everyone on the wagon train had told her. Yesterday, Hiram Fredericks had proudly explained that the fort provided travelers, explorers and, occasionally, the U.S. Army, with a place to obtain supplies, livestock, food, fresh water, as well as rest and relaxation.

There was a bell tower and bastions at opposite corners of the fort that were used for lookout posts and for storage. Each bastion was armed with a cannon. Fredericks had explained that, so far, they'd never been used for defense, but for signals and to welcome important people, a fact that Lily was pleased to hear.

The fort housed much the same things as a small town: a kitchen, dining room, blacksmith and carpenter shop, warehouses and, of course, the trade room. Lily wasn't sure what was upstairs on the second floor of the fort, other than more living quarters and the billiard room Fredericks had mentioned last night.

What Lily did know, for certain, was that the fort was populated mostly by men.

She kept her eyes forward as she walked, but felt the gazes of the men upon her. They paused in midstride. They stopped their chores, their conversations. Their faces appeared in windows and doorways.

Men. Big men. Frightening-looking men. Wild hair and unkempt beards. Buckskins stained with sweat. Faces lined with wind and sun. Trappers, mountain men, hunters, prospectors, explorers, adventurers.

A new awareness came with Lily's every step, her

every movement. The sway of her skirt, the rustle of her petticoats, the tug of the breeze in her hair, the fabric of her collar against her throat.

Lily glanced around. Where was Mrs. Nelson? Surely other women were here at the fort. Where were they?

A fear, a vulnerability settled in the pit of Lily's stomach. Outnumbered. Overmatched. A lamb among the wolves.

She considered rushing back to her room, closing herself up inside, bolting the door, but Mr. Sykes had asked her to leave while he examined her father. She couldn't burst in unannounced. What would he think of her if she walked in at an inappropriate moment?

Lily kept walking, dozens of gazes tracking her steps. She held her chin up, feigning a leisurely stroll, then darted through the passageway near the carpenter's shop and into the alley behind.

No men.

She waited and held her breath as she watched the passageway. No one followed.

Relieved, Lily eased between the wooden crates and barrels stacked in the shade of the building, and found a spot to sit down. Hidden in the clutter, she felt somewhat safe and secure.

Across the alley, a horse was tethered to the corral fence at the corner of the stable. It stamped the ground, stirring up little dust clouds, and tossed its head fitfully, pulling at the rope.

The animal was no more comfortable at the fort than she was, Lily thought.

She sat back, trying to get comfortable, trying to relax, willing herself to shake the feeling of foreboding that still hung over her like a dark cloud, and turned her thoughts to her aunt in Richmond.

What would Aunt Maribel be doing at this exact moment? she wondered, turning her face skyward to catch the sun.

Or better still, what if Lily had talked her father out of making this trip altogether? Yes, that was a better fantasy, she decided. He'd be well and healthy, going about his business, as usual, in Saint Louis.

But the prospect of how different her life would be at this very moment if she'd gone to visit her wealthy aunt instead of making this trip, came unbidden into Lily's mind once more.

She sighed quietly, indulging herself in the imaginary scene her mind conjured up.

She'd have spent her first week in her aunt's lovely home getting acclimated to the new house, recovering from the journey, learning about the city. She'd luxuriate in a steaming tub, nap often, and be fawned over by a parade of maids and servants. Then preparations for the social outings to come would commence. Fabrics and patterns discussed, new gowns commissioned. The parties, teas and luncheons given in her honor to introduce her and welcome her to the city would take weeks, all amid ladies and gentlemen of good breeding and impeccable deportment.

Yet here she sat on a wooden crate, civilization but a distant memory, with the vague odor of animal manure in the air.

Lily settled her feet onto a lower crate and wrapped her arms around her knees. Another wave of loneliness washed over her. She'd never felt so isolated in her life. So vulnerable. So lost.

Tears pushed at the backs of her eyes, but she forced them down. If she allowed one single tear to fall, a torrent would follow—and she hadn't thought to bring a handkerchief with her. Madame DuBois would be appalled.

The stallion tethered to the corral across the alley tossed its head and nickered, its eyes widening to circles of white. Fighting the lead rope, it pulled back, pawing at the earth. The animal was young and strong, a fine specimen of horseflesh. Lily knew he'd fetch a fine price—if he didn't injure himself trying to escape.

A man appeared at the corner of the stable inside the corral. He wore trousers and a pale-blue shirt, with a black hat pulled low on his forehead that shaded his face.

Had she seen this man yesterday? Lily wondered.

Something about him seemed familiar. Was he the man tending the brown mare she'd glimpsed as she'd spoken with Mr. Fredericks? The only man in the entire fort who hadn't walked over to gawk at her?

A gasp slipped from Lily's lips when she saw him headed toward the stallion. She almost called out a warning, but his slow, relaxed steps stopped her.

Low on the breeze, his voice came to her, a rumbling whisper. She couldn't understand the words, but the tone was mesmerizing. The stallion thought so, too, apparently. As Lily watched, the man continued to speak softly as he inched closer, and by the time he reached the horse, it had settled down.

Still murmuring quietly, the man patted the horse's neck and brought its big head against his chest. The stallion stood quietly.

Awe and mystery stirred in Lily. How had the man done that? Gentled the horse with nothing more than his words? She'd never seen anything like it.

Patting the stallion, the man turned his back to Lily. She gasped aloud. Straight, jet-black hair hung past his shoulders.

Indian.

A rush of emotion swept through Lily. Fear, apprehension, curiosity.

Everyone on the wagon train had warned her about these Indians, their savagery, their heinous acts, the atrocities they committed—things so vile men wouldn't whisper them to a decent woman.

Yet this Indian seemed anything but menacing, despite his size. Tall, broad shouldered with thick arms and a lean waist. His pressed, well-mended clothing was the cleanest she'd seen at the fort.

And he had gentled the stallion. With words and measured actions, he'd not only brought the horse under control, but calmed it as well.

Sitting perfectly still on the crate, Lily watched as the breeze pulled at the man's shirt and ruffled his black hair. One evening on the wagon train she'd spoken with a young woman who'd told her that Indian men had no hair on their chests. For the first time, Lily's stomach tingled at the notion. Could it be true?

She'd seen a bare-chested man a few times in her life. On the journey west when the men of the wagon train had been forced to engage in some difficult work in the heat of the day, they'd occasionally taken off their shirts.

But what would a smooth chest look like?

Beneath the fabric of his shirt, muscles bunched, expanded, contracted. Were they bare? she wondered. Smooth, slick—

The Indian turned sharply, his gaze finding her on the crates and pinning her there.

Lily gulped. Good gracious! He'd caught her staring. Could he possibly know that she'd been think-ing about his chest—of all things?

She shrank deeper into the crates, drawing her legs up under her. Humiliation burned her cheeks. How unseemly of her. How unladylike. Ogling a man. Wondering about his chest. Madame DuBois would indeed be appalled.

Desperate to escape the hiding place that had sud-denly become a prison, Lily froze as she heard foot-steps. Easing around the edge of the crate, she saw a man—this one rail thin with blond hair—walking from the passageway beside the carpenter's shop to-ward the corral.

She'd not seen this man before. Lily was sure she would have remembered. His buckskins hung loose on his thin frame, blond hair streaked with gray lay across his shoulders, a heavy mustache drooped past his lips. His hat shaded most of his lined face.

The Indian saw him, too, watched as he ap-proached. He'd not seen *her* at all, Lily realized. It was the blond-haired man who'd drawn his atten-tion.

The two men faced each other through the corral fence, a contrast of tall and muscular, thin and stooped. Neither smiled. They didn't shake hands. A few words were exchanged, but Lily couldn't hear them.

The Indian glanced up and down the alley, then pulled something from his trouser pocket—a packet of papers, a wad of money, perhaps?—and passed it to the other man. He shoved it in his own pocket and walked away. The Indian glanced around once more, then turned and disappeared behind the stable.

Lily waited for a moment, the feeling of foreboding that had plagued her for so long growing stronger—but for a very different reason this time. Just as the Indian had done, she checked around to see if anyone was watching, then slipped quietly from her hiding place among the crates and hurried back to her room.

"There's just no easy way to say this, ma'am," Oliver Sykes said, ducking his head, refusing to make eye contact with Lily.

"What?" She looked back and forth between Sykes and Hiram Fredericks, both men grim faced and solemn. "What is it?"

Standing outside the door to her room, Lily gazed at the evening shadows stretched across the plaza bringing a cooling breeze with the disappearing sun. Sykes had come by to see her father again, then left and had just now returned with Fredericks. They'd called her outside.

"Your pa's bad off, I reckon you know that," Fredericks finally said.

"But he's getting better," Lily insisted. "He slept straight through the night, and he's been resting quietly all day. He's—"

''No, ma'am, that's not so,'' Sykes said with fatherly kindness.

''Yes, it is,'' Lily told them. Why were these two men saying such things? She wanted them to leave. ''Now, I must go back inside and see to my father—''

''He's dying.'' Fredericks closed his hand over her arm, holding her in place. ''The fever took its toll.''

''It was just too much for him,'' Sykes added. He paused, then added, ''Your pa probably won't make it through the night.''

Tears sprang to Lily's eyes. ''No…''

''He roused up a bit a while ago,'' Sykes said. ''He's asking for you.''

Lily shook her head, her throat tight and thick. ''But…''

''Go on inside,'' Fredericks said kindly. He guided Lily into the room, then closed the door behind her.

Lily clung to the door, afraid to cross the room, afraid to approach the cot. Her father couldn't be dying. Fredericks and Sykes meant well, but they had to be wrong—they simply had to be.

''No, Papa, you can't—you simply can't,'' she whispered. ''Not now. We haven't even…''

But her father lay so still, awash in a gray, ghostly pallor, that she knew the men were right. Tears sprang to her eyes. Lily covered her face with her palms.

"Lily…?"

Her head jerked up at the sound of Augustus's voice. She rushed to his bedside and dropped to her knees, joy filling her heart.

"Yes, Papa?" she said anxiously. "Oh, I knew you wouldn't—"

"It's…gone," he whispered.

Lily frowned. "What—whatever do you mean?"

With effort, Augustus lifted his head from the sweat-stained pillow, but collapsed again, his lips moving as if trying to speak.

Lily leaned closer, her ear to his mouth. "What, Papa? What is it?"

"Money…" he whispered. "All…gone."

She looked at him, unable to follow his reasoning. Why was he talking about money—of all things— at a time like this?

"Bad deals…lost it all…nothing left." Augustus drew in a ragged breath, then wheezed. "That's… that's why I came West…to…to start over."

"No, Papa," Lily insisted. "That's not true. You told me yourself that you'd always wanted to come West, to explore, to seek new adventures."

His head moved back and forth with effort. "A lie. I told you that so…" He coughed. "Thought I could make my fortune over again...in Santa Fe. Thought I could..."

"But, Papa—"

Augustus's eyelids sank.

"Papa? Papa!"

Chapter Three

Lily stood beside the mound of fresh-turned earth and the wooden casket that would be her father's resting place for eternity, cold despite the heat of the midafternoon sun that bore down on them.

Augustus had passed away peacefully in his sleep during the night, just as Oliver Sykes had predicted, with Lily at his side.

Hiram Fredericks had made the funeral arrangements; he seemed to be in charge of such things, much like everything else at the fort.

Oliver Sykes, who had worked diligently to heal her father, had arranged for his casket to be built, then had laid him in it. Lily didn't know who'd dug the grave, here among the other wooden markers outside the fort.

Fredericks read from the Bible, the thin pages rattling in the breeze, his white hair undulating on the unseen current. About a dozen men—most of whom

Lily didn't know—gathered there also. She wondered if they wanted to pay their respects, or simply craved a diversion from their daily routine.

Jacob Tanner, the young man who worked in the kitchen and had brought meal trays to her and her father, stood near the back of the gathering, his hands clasped in front of him, his eyes lowered respectfully. Lily appreciated his presence and felt his intentions were honorable.

Not in attendance was the Nelson family, the people her papa had paid to drive their wagon and assist them in their journey. Nor were the men from the wagon train, who'd come with them to the fort, present for the service.

Lily sniffed, choking back tears—bitter tears. Augustus deserved so much more at his passing. The presence of his friends and business associates in Saint Louis who really knew him and would have truly mourned his death. A carved, marble marker befitting a man of his stature, rather than a simple wooden cross. Men—knowledgeable men—who would have stepped in.

Someone who would tell Lily what was to become of her now.

She touched her finger to the corner of her eye, catching another tear. In the plain wooden casket lay her father. More of a stranger to her now than she'd ever imagined. She'd thought she knew what sort of man he was, but after his deathbed confession last night, she obviously did not.

Could it be true? she wondered as Fredericks's reading of Bible verses droned on. Had Augustus really lost their entire family fortune?

Sitting at his bedside last night, hearing his confession, Lily had thought it was simply more of his nonsensical fevered ramblings. He'd been incoherent for days. He'd talked to people who weren't there, flailed his arms against unseen foes. Surely something in his dying mind had prompted this delusion, fabricated the loss of his business empire.

But didn't the mere fact that they were here in this forsaken wilderness give credence to his confession? Her father had lived his entire life in a large comfortable home, waited on by a number of servants, his every need catered to by others. When he'd told Lily of his dream to go West and explore new lands, she'd thought it odd. So unlike him.

Yet it made perfect sense if he'd indeed lost all his money and wanted to start over in Santa Fe.

It also explained why he'd been so reluctant to have Lily accompany him on this trip.

Other thoughts floated through Lily's mind as the men, gathered around her father's gravesite, sang a hymn.

Last Christmas she'd wanted to travel to Memphis to spend the holiday with her friend's family. Augustus had told her no. When she'd asked for funds to commission several new gowns, he'd never sent the money; she thought he'd simply forgotten. Just before her graduation, he'd appeared unexpectedly at her boarding school and met privately with Madame DuBois. Now Lily wondered if there had been a problem with her tuition; that would explain why some of the other girls had whispered behind their hands as Lily passed them in the halls.

Fredericks gently touched Lily's arm and she realized the service had ended. The men nodded toward her, putting on their hats, respectfully touching the brims, then drifted away. Jacob lingered a moment as if he wanted to say something to her, but finally he wandered away after only a respectful nod.

"Thank you," she managed to say, her voice tight, barely more than a ragged whisper. She fought off another swell of emotion. "Thank you very much, both of you, for arranging everything."

Oliver Sykes, standing on the other side of her, nodded. "It was a nice turnout."

"I thought the Nelsons would be here," Lily said, gazing around as if she might see them. "They helped us all along the journey. We'd gotten to know them quite well, I'd thought."

"Oh, they left already," Sykes said.

"Left?" Lily looked back and forth between the two men, an odd feeling tightening her belly. "What do you mean they left?"

"Gone on to Santa Fe," Sykes explained. "Them and those other fellas from the wagon train who drove in with you. They all left at dawn."

"But…" Stunned, Lily just gazed at the men. They'd gone? Left her behind? Abandoned her in this place? Without so much as a farewell wave?

"But my father paid the Nelson family to look after us," Lily said, desperation creeping into her voice. "They're supposed to do the cooking, drive the wagon, take care of the horses."

The two men exchanged a troubled look that squeezed Lily's stomach into a tight knot.

"This isn't hardly the best time, right here at your father's funeral, but I guess you've got to be told." Sykes pulled at the back of his neck. "I mean, you'll find out, sooner or later."

Lily pressed her lips together, afraid to ask what he was talking about.

"Last night…" Fredericks cleared his throat. "Well, last night, your horses were stolen."

"Stolen?"

"Yeah, and your wagon was looted." Sykes shifted uncomfortably. "Pretty much everything you had in there is gone. The wagon was torn up, too."

Her horses were stolen? Her belongings stolen? Lily pressed her hand to her forehead as the world suddenly pitched sideways.

She was penniless—*and* stranded?

"Who—who did it? Who's responsible?" she asked.

Fredericks shrugged. "Don't know. Sam Becker—he's the blacksmith—he saw what had happened to your wagon this morning, then went to check on your horses and realized they were gone."

"Shouldn't we report this to someone?" Lily asked, spreading her hands.

"Well, Miss St. Claire, it's not like we got a real lawman here at the fort," Sykes said.

"Me and the boys, well, we just take care of things as they come up, best we can," Fredericks explained. "Becker said he didn't have any idea who might have taken your belongings."

"I—I'd like to go lie down," Lily gasped, feeling light-headed.

"That's a good idea," Fredericks said.

"Yeah, good idea," Sykes agreed, as if he were glad to be rid of her.

"I'll walk with you—" Fredericks began.

"No." Lily pulled away from him. "No, thank you. I can manage."

Though she wasn't sure that she could, Lily somehow made it to her room and closed the door tight behind her. She fell back against it, her heart thudding in her chest, her mind whirling.

Her horses and her belongings were gone. Her wagon damaged. *And* she had no money.

Without cash how would she buy horses? How would she repair the wagon, let alone reprovision it?

How would she ever escape this dreadful land?

Lily pressed her fingers to her lips, holding back a sob. What would become of her?

Her gaze landed on the cot across the room, the cot on which only yesterday her father had lain, then died. She'd never felt so alone.

Bile rose in the back of her throat, closing off her breathing in this airless room.

She had to leave. She had to escape. She couldn't abide this room—this fort—another moment.

Lily opened the door and slipped out of the fort into the prairie.

North paused outside the trade room as he glimpsed a swish of skirt disappear out the gate. Even without seeing her face he knew it was Lily St. Claire, the woman whose father they'd just buried. No other woman wore that sort of dress.

And no other woman would be foolish enough to leave the safety of the fort.

North shook his head. Why would she do this? Didn't she know any better?

Or did she simply not care that she was a danger not only to herself, but to others who might have to go after her?

Since arriving at the fort she'd been waited on hand and foot, seemingly unable to accomplish the

smallest task, or fend for herself. Was this customary behavior for white women?

North recalled the stories his father had told about
women in the East, his mother, sisters, aunts, left
behind like all his other family members. Women
so unlike North's own Cheyenne mother, his sisters
and the other women of the tribe.

North waited and watched the gate. No one else,
apparently, had seen Lily leave. The routine of the
fort continued on, as usual. Minutes dragged by. The
sun drifted toward the Western horizon.

He watched. Still no sign of her.

He hoped she'd realize that the prairie was no
place for her and come back on her own. He waited
longer. She didn't return.

North glanced around. No one, still, had noticed
that she was gone. That meant he'd have no choice
but to go after her himself.

He hesitated. Something about that woman bothered him. He didn't know what it was, exactly. He
couldn't quite put his finger on it. But it was there,
lurking in the back of his mind, and in the pit of his
stomach.

''Damn…''

North headed for the stable.

A dark shadow fell across the ground startling
Lily. She gasped and twisted around. A man stood

behind her, his approach so silent she hadn't heard a sound.

Seated on the ground, Lily brushed the tears from her eyes, then shaded them against the setting sun, squinting to see his face.

"Who are you?" she asked, unwilling and unable to sound pleasant.

He didn't reply, just looked down at her quizzically.

Lily leaned her head back to see him clearly. He was the Indian she'd seen whispering to the stallion in the corral, she realized.

She gazed past him and the horse he'd left grazing a few yards away, to Bent's Fort, now small on the horizon. She hadn't realized she'd gone so far. She'd walked—then run—through the short, green prairie grass to the river, then followed its banks, finally collapsing here beneath a cottonwood tree, mindless of the distance.

She didn't know why this man was here or what he wanted—and she didn't care, either. All she wanted was to be left alone to cry, to scream, to indulge the ache in her heart and the emptiness in her soul. Was that too much to ask? Surely it couldn't be, after what she'd been through today.

"Go away," she told him, turning away, tears filling her eyes once more. "I want to be by myself. I don't want any company. Can't you understand that's why I came out here in the first place?"

He walked closer, still staring down at her. Though he'd said nothing, his presence seemed to demand something of her.

"This has been the worst day of my life. Everything—absolutely everything—has been just awful. Why, I didn't even have anything decent to wear to my own father's funeral." Lily shook the skirt of her green dress, the simple act bringing on another rush of emotion and a fresh wave of tears. "Why, I—I—I don't even have a handkerchief!"

The magnitude of her woes descended upon her, crushing her. She sobbed into her hands, not bothering to hide her tears or wipe them away.

"My horses were stolen!" she wailed, turning her face up to him. "My belongings, too! My wagon is ruined! And I don't have any money!"

She flung herself onto the ground and cradled her head against her arms, sobbing and gulping in ragged breaths of air.

Lily glanced up. The man still stood over her, his head tilted slightly to the side, watching her as if she were an insect in a jar.

"Is that all you can do?" she demanded. "Stand there and stare?"

His brows drew together, but still he didn't offer a response.

She pushed herself up and huffed irritably. "Don't you have any manners at all?"

His frown deepened.

"Do you speak English?" she wanted to know. When he didn't answer, she asked again. "Eng...lish. Do...you...speak...English?"

The man rocked back slightly, regarding her with caution.

"Oh, lovely!" Lily dug the heels of her shoes into the ground and launched herself to her feet. "Here I am pouring out my heart to someone who doesn't even speak a civilized language!"

She whirled away and flung out both arms. "What sort of godforsaken place is this? Savages running loose! With no sense of decorum! No manners! Unable to even communicate!"

"What's wrong with it?"

Lily gasped at the sound of his voice, and spun toward him. Embarrassment heated her cheeks. "You *do* speak English."

He watched her curiously. "Your dress. What's wrong with it?"

Lily planted a hand on her hip and pushed her chin up. "You should have made your language skills known earlier, sir, and not allowed me to carry on like that. And you should have introduced yourself."

"North Walker," he said, seemingly unperturbed by her scathing accusations about his heritage. "Your father has just died. Yet your concern is with your dress?"

"It's the wrong color," she told him and shook

her skirt once more. "It should be black, not green. Black is always worn to a funeral—in civilized places, that is. And, of course, I'm upset about my father's death."

Tears filled Lily's eyes again. Emotion swelled in her, robbing her of her strength. She sank to the ground, her skirt pooling around her, not wanting to put forth the effort to stand.

"We were supposed to be a family—finally—on this trip. But now Papa's gone, and I'm alone. All alone," she whispered. Tears tumbled down her cheeks once more. She covered her face with her hands. "This was our last chance...our last chance to be together." After a few minutes, she sensed North move closer, his nearness somehow calming her emotions.

"Your father is dead," North said softly, kneeling beside her. "Gone to a better place."

Lily sniffed and lifted her head.

"Isn't that your belief?" North asked gently. "That he's in heaven among the angels, free of pain and suffering, in the presence of the Holy Spirit?"

"You're a Christian?" She swiped the tears from her face with the backs of her hands, unable to keep the surprise from her voice.

"I know God." North waved his hand encompassing everything around them. "I know the spirit of the land and all things in it."

"But—but you're an *Indian?*"

"I'm a lot of things," he told her.

North closed his hand over her arm. Heat seeped through the fabric of her sleeve, oozing outward, filling her with warmth.

He looked directly into her eyes. "Your father is at peace. Rejoice in his place in heaven. Don't wish him into the torment of this earth again."

Lily gazed into his eyes—rich, dark eyes that seemed to peer into her soul and, somehow, lift her burden. Almost magically, a sense of peace filled her. Her problems drifted away as if they were feathers on the breeze.

"Thank you for your kindness," she whispered. "You've made me feel so much better."

"It's the same way I talk to my horses." North rose and said. "But horses have more sense than to come out onto the prairie alone and get themselves in such a dangerous situation."

It took a few seconds before his words sank in.

"Are you saying I don't have as much sense as a *horse?*" she demanded. Lily scrambled to her feet. "How dare you! You don't even know me, nor do you have the slightest idea of what sort of person I am, yet you have the gall to stand there and—"

"We have to go back to the fort," he said and reached for her arm.

Lily jerked away. "I have no intention of going anywhere with you."

"It's a longer walk back than you think. It will be dark soon."

She squared her shoulders, a strength she hadn't felt a moment ago suddenly filling her. "I'll manage, thank you just the same."

He gestured toward the horizon and the orange glow of the setting sun. "Coyotes prowl at sundown. There're snakes."

Lily drew in a great breath. "I'll go back to the fort when I choose. And I'll get there on my own."

"You won't make it," North said, anger creeping into his voice. "Most of the men at the fort will end up out here searching for you, risking their own lives."

And she wasn't worth it, his look seemed to say.

A sickly feeling wound through Lily's stomach, shame that this man thought so little of her. Memories of the weeks on the Trail came back to her, the other women caring for their families, tending to them with practiced ease. She'd been unprepared for the journey. She'd known it from the start. She still knew it. But, somehow, seeing that look on North's face hurt worst of all.

"I don't need your help," Lily said, holding up her chin.

A long moment dragged by while North just looked at her. Finally, he simply nodded.

"Fine," he said, then mounted his horse and headed toward the fort.

Lily gasped and her eyes rounded at the sight of him riding away. He was leaving her? Actually riding away? Abandoning her here so far from the fort, in the middle of nowhere?

"Wait!" She ran after him. "Stop!"

She caught up with him. North rested his hand on the saddle horn and glared down, the brim of his hat shading his eyes.

"You're—you're not going to *leave* me out here, are you?" she exclaimed. She drew herself up, thinking of the nastiest thing she could call him. "You, Mr. Walker, are no gentleman."

He gave her a long, slow once-over that sent a strange warmth flooding through her. Heat crept up her neck and onto her cheeks, then arrowed downward to the center of her belly. Still, Lily refused to look away.

Finally, North shook his head, almost to himself, and climbed down from the horse.

Relieved, but still clinging to her pride, Lily said, "I decided that it would be prudent to accept your offer and—Oh!"

North grasped her waist and hoisted her upward, plopping her into the saddle. Lily grasped a handful of mane to keep from tumbling backward off the other side, then glared down at him. He glared right back.

An odd warmth leaped from him, covered her, touched her in strange places. She'd assumed he thought her worthless, but the look on his face made her feel as if—

Lily broke eye contact, afraid—but of what she wasn't sure.

North picked up the reins, then reached into his trouser pocket and pulled out his handkerchief. He held it up to Lily.

Stunned, she looked at it for a moment. The white, pressed linen fabric. His big hard long fingers. She'd complained earlier that she had no handkerchief. He'd remembered.

Without a word, Lily accepted it. North led the horse toward the fort.

In the moonlight the fort looked almost pleasant, Lily thought as she gazed out the window of her room. She rested her arm on the sill, looking up at the stars, searching them for—

What? A glimpse into the future? A window into her own heart?

When they'd drawn close to the fort this evening, Lily had jumped from the horse, marched right past North and entered the fort alone. She'd hurried to her room, not bothering to even thank him.

Not that he deserved to be thanked, after the way he'd insulted her.

Yet it was her pride that hurt more than anything. He thought little of her, and she'd done nothing to prove him wrong.

But what was she to do? She didn't belong in this place, was totally unprepared for life here in the un-civilized West. Yet, somehow, North's low opinion of her still hurt.

Sighing into the dark night, Lily decided this was but further proof that she should leave immediately for her aunt's home in Richmond.

She'd be glad to go. She'd miss nothing about this hard, unforgiving land. The land that had taken her father and the last chance she'd ever have to know what it was like for the two of them to be a family.

North floated through her mind. Tall, wide shoulders. So strong. He'd lifted her into the saddle with no effort. And he was handsome, surprisingly handsome. When Oliver Sykes had stopped by her room to check on her a short while ago, she'd casually— she hoped—asked about North. An English father and a Cheyenne mother, Sykes had said. His mixed heritage had blended to give him a unique handsomeness, to Lily's mind.

Her stomach warmed at the memory of the two of them beneath the cottonwood tree. He belonged here in this land. He was strong and brave and rugged. Everything this place demanded.

And she wasn't. A thread of sadness filled Lily's heart at the thought. Then alarm took its place.

North had seemed decent enough under the cottonwood. But he was, after all, half-Indian. Half-savage. What if his Cheyenne side had presented itself at that particular moment? Would he have ravished her? Scalped her? Left her for dead?

A chill ran up Lily's spine. She had to leave this place. Tomorrow she'd make the arrangements.

She'd get to her aunt's home in Virginia—no matter what it took.

Chapter Four

Gray clouds hung over the fort, stretching to the horizon, heavy with the threat of rain. The morning breeze tugged at the loose strands of Lily's hair as she crossed the plaza.

She stepped inside the trade room, the economic heart of Bent's Fort, the primary reason for its existence in this vast wilderness. Here, merchandise, goods and services were traded or sold to Indians and trappers, travelers and explorers.

As she hoped, Lily found Hiram Fredericks and Oliver Sykes busy at work among the dry goods, hardware, tools, guns and knives.

The two of them had done so much to help her these past few days, they deserved her thanks and so very much more. That was, however, all that she could offer these two fine gentlemen, in light of her newly discovered financial straits.

"Good morning," she greeted, and managed a small smile as she cross the room.

Both men looked up from the desk they were huddled around, and smiled in return, looking a little surprised but pleased to see her.

"How're you doing, Miss St. Claire?" Sykes inquired, giving her an earnest look, setting aside the stack of papers in his hand.

"Well enough," she said, trying to push her chin up a little and sound brave, "considering the circumstances, of course."

"Of course," Fredericks agreed.

"Could I trouble you gentlemen for a little information?" Lily asked, pushing on.

"Sure thing," Sykes told her and leaned forward just a little.

"How soon before one might expect a wagon train to come up from Santa Fe, through the fort, bound for the East?" Lily asked.

Wagons routinely made the journey east from Santa Fe, loaded with handwoven blankets, buffalo robes, furs and other riches that would be sold in Eastern markets. The trade route worked both ways.

"Oh, we get wagons through here every week or so. Sometimes more often than that." Sykes glanced at Fredericks for confirmation.

"Yeah, about that often, I'd say," Fredericks agreed, stroking his chin.

"Fine," Lily said, a sense of relief coming over

her. "I'll join the next wagon train that passes through heading east."

She'd thought about it most of the night, tossing and turning on the little cot in her room, then pacing across the floor and staring out the window, until she'd come up with a plan.

While she had no money to pay her way east, she did own a wagon—albeit a damaged wagon—which was surely worth something and could be offered in trade. If that failed, she could provide a service of some sort to the travelers. Take care of young children, perhaps, or act as a schoolmarm on the trip. She could give art instruction, read books or poetry.

If, of course, any sort of payment was required. Surely, the people of the train would appreciate her plight and allow her to travel with them.

Fredericks nodded his understanding. "Seems like leaving is the sensible thing to do. I mean, for a woman like you, that is."

He'd said it kindly enough, but an insult lurked there just the same. Lily felt its sting, yet couldn't disagree.

"Would you be kind enough to let me know when the next wagon comes through, so I can be on my way?" she asked the men.

"Sure thing, Miss St. Claire. You can head on back East any time you like," Fredericks said. His expression hardened. "As soon as you settle your debts here, of course."

She blinked up at him. "My…debts?"

Fredericks and Sykes nodded in unison.

"Hiram's got it all writ down, nice and neat," Sykes said, and wagged his finger toward Fredericks and the desk. "Show her the ledger, Hiram."

"Ledger…?" Her stomach jerked into a knot. "But I thought—"

"Thought what?" Sykes asked, and gave her a hard look. He shifted closer. "You didn't think all this stuff here was free, did you?"

A rush of embarrassment—and panic—coursed through Lily.

Fredericks pushed aside some papers on his desk, searching until he found the ledger. He opened it and flipped through the pages.

"Here we go, Miss St. Claire," he said, finding the spot. "I got a whole page, just for you."

Lily gulped. "A whole page?"

"Now, first off," he said, holding the ledger at arm's length, "there's meals. Three a day, every day you were here, plus the cost of bringing them to your room. And meals for your pa, of course."

"But Papa didn't even eat—"

"Then there's the laundry you wanted done," Fredericks said, running his finger along the page, "and the cost of your room. An extra charge for two people together, of course."

"Papa was sick," Lily implored. "I needed to be at his side—"

"Doctor's expenses," Fredericks went on. "Two visits a day, at your request. Medicine, bandages, that sort of thing."

Footsteps, shuffling feet sounded behind Lily and she sensed other men coming into the room, adding to her embarrassment.

"Then there's board and care for your horses," Fredericks said.

"My horses were stolen!"

"That don't mean they didn't eat while they were here," Sykes pointed out.

"And then there's storage on your wagon," Mr. Fredericks continued.

"It was ransacked!"

Fredericks paused, and he and Sykes looked at each other as if considering the point she'd just made.

"Somebody get Sam over here," Sykes called over Lily's head, then said to her, "Sam Becker. He's the blacksmith that took care of your horses and wagon."

She glanced behind her and saw one of the men lean out the door and yell.

"Let's see now, what else?" Fredericks squinted at the page. "Oh, yeah. There's the funeral. Making the casket, digging the grave, of course, carving your pa's name into the cross."

"I did the carving myself," Sykes said to Lily

and grinned proudly. "Thought it was a nice touch, if I do say so myself."

"Well, I guess that's about it. So there you have it. That's everything," Fredericks announced, closing the ledger with a snap. "As soon as you pay up, Miss St. Claire, you're free to be on your way."

Lily's breath came in quick little heaves, making her heart pounded harder in her chest. She owed these men money? A lot of money? And they wouldn't let her leave this retched place until she paid them?

"But—but I don't have any money," Lily said, spreading her hands.

The two men exchanged a troubled look, then both shook their heads.

"Well, now," Sykes said. "I guess we got ourselves a problem."

"I guess we do," Fredericks agreed.

A little murmur went through the gathering of men situated behind Lily. They'd overheard every word spoken in the room, knew it was a private conversation, yet they'd stayed as if she and her plight were their morning entertainment. Lily's embarrassment deepened.

Fredericks looked up suddenly and smiled broadly. "Morning, Sam. Come on in here."

Sam Becker, the blacksmith, murmured a greeting to the men in the room, then shouldered his way past Lily to stand beside Fredericks and Sykes.

She'd seen him around the fort, but had never been introduced. He was young, short, thick chested, with muscular arms and meaty hands. He was always sweating.

Fredericks opened the ledger once more, then gave Becker a rundown on Lily's situation. Becker looked over the older man's shoulder and nodded.

"I don't think it's fair that I be charged for boarding my horses when they were stolen while in your care," Lily said, trying to remain calm.

Becker looked up at Lily and dragged the back of his hand across his damp brow, leaving a smudged trail of dirt all the way across. He shrugged. "Knock a dollar off my bill," he said to Fredericks.

"A dollar?" Lily gasped.

Fredericks made a notation in the ledger, then presented it to Lily. "There's your total, Miss St. Claire."

Her eyes widened. She felt light-headed. It was a fortune. An absolute fortune. How would she ever manage to pay it?

"I—I have the wagon," she said and heard the desperation in her own voice. "Would you take that in trade?"

Fredericks and Sykes turned to Becker. He shook his head.

"That wagon of yours ain't worth what it'd take to roll it off a cliff," he said to Lily, shaking his head sadly. "Whoever stole your stuff ripped the canvas all to hell— Pardon me for saying so, ma'am. It's tore up real bad on the inside, too. Running gear's not much better.''

"But what about my belongings?" Lily offered hopefully. "Surely the vandals left *something* of value I could trade with."

Becker shrugged. "All that's left inside is a bunch of fancy dresses, some dishes, books—nothing that's worth nothing."

"Those dresses were designed and sewn by the finest seamstress in the East," Lily insisted. "And the china is a pattern designed specifically for my family, sent all the way from—"

"You got anything of real value?" Fredericks asked her, cutting her off. "Tools? Whiskey?"

"Well…no," Lily admitted.

"Huh…" Fredericks stroked his chin and looked back and forth between Sykes and Becker. "What you reckon we ought to do with her?" he asked them.

The three men gazed at Lily and it took all her willpower not to blush.

"How's your cooking?" Sykes asked.

"Well, I don't actually cook," Lily said, then forced a hopeful smile. "I *supervise* cooks."

Fredericks shook his head. "You got any sort of a trade?"

"No, not exactly," Lily admitted.

"Well, what *can* you do?" Becker asked, looking her up and down.

"I can paint—I'm especially gifted with watercolors—and I embroider," Lily announced. She drew herself up straighter. "I can plan a party for a hundred people, supervise a large domestic staff—"

"We're not planning to have no parties any time soon," Sykes said.

"And our domestic staff?" Becker said. "We gave them the summer off."

A round of chuckles erupted from the men gathered in the trade room behind Lily. She blushed red, the heat burning her cheeks.

The laughter was followed by a long, uncomfortable silence as the three men continued to look at Lily, assessing her value.

"She can't do anything," Fredericks proclaimed, sounding the death kneel on Lily's worth. "She's too small to do any real work, she's got no trade, no skills."

Becker and Sykes nodded in agreement.

Lily's embarrassment deepened because they were right. She really was of no value here in the West.

Yet might that work in her favor? Hope sprang in Lily's thoughts. Since she was so obviously of no value to anyone here at the fort, would they simply let her leave, let her go on her way, knowing they couldn't possibly recoup their money?

"I know people—wealthy people—in Saint Louis," Lily said, her spirits lifting. "If you'll just let me leave here, I'll send your money back—every penny—as soon as I set foot in the city. I swear I will."

"Naw," Fredericks said, shaking his head. "That's not a good idea."

"How do we know you'd really send it?" Sykes proposed, then added, "No offense, Miss St. Claire."

"We need the money before you leave," Fredericks said, announcing it with a finality that caused Lily's stomach to jerk into a tighter knot.

Lily's mind spun. Her father's business associates, friends in Saint Louis would send the money to her here at the fort. Aunt Maribel would gladly do the same. But it would take weeks—months, even—for her message requesting the money to be delivered and the funds sent to her here at the fort.

Revulsion tightened around her heart. She couldn't—absolutely could not—stay at this fort for that length of time.

Mr. Sykes looked at her one more time, then sighed heavily and said, "Well, I guess there's only one thing we can do."

Lily's hopes soared. She leaned forward trying to hear the three men as they crowded together and whispered. She prayed—desperately—that the men would take pity on her and simply let her leave.

"All right, then, it's settled," Sykes said when the huddle broke up. "Here's what we've decided to do for you, Miss St. Claire. We've decided to set you up in business, right here at the fort."

"Business?" Lily asked, stunned.

"Makes sense. Good sense," Becker said, eyeing her critically, seeming to see her a little differently now. "After all, you're just about the only white woman around these parts."

Alarm spread through Lily. "What sort of business?"

Sykes shrugged. "You're a pretty little thing, even if you can't do much."

"What sort of business?"

"Here's how we'll work things," Fredericks explained. "We'll give you a room here in the fort. Once word gets out, well shoot, I expect we'll have men lined up all the way out the gate."

"Are you suggesting that I become a—a—" Lily struggled to find her breath. "A—prostitute?"

"You got any better idea?" Sykes asked.

Raw fear raced through Lily. She backed up and turned, looking for an escape. But more men had come into the trade room and were blocking the door. And every one of them leered at her, as if contemplating her naked.

"I—I can't possibly…" she said, shaking her head frantically.

"We'll give you a break on your room rent," Fredericks told her.

"N-no, I can't—"

"Then you'd better figure some other way to come up with the cash you owe us," Sykes told her.

"There must be something else you can do," Lily insisted. "Please, I can't—"

"Get her a room close to the kitchen," Becker suggested. "More convenient that way."

"And I'll put up a sign," Sykes offered.

"Paint it red," Becker advised.

"No!" Lily insisted.

"Don't worry," Fredericks said. "You'll pay off your debts in a couple months' time."

"Listen to me." Lily clenched her fists. "You can't force me to do this."

"Then how are you going to pay us?" Fredericks demanded, his voice growing angry. "Do you think you can just waltz in here with your high-handed Eastern ways, take everything at your pleasure, then leave like none of it happened? You'll do as we say, and that's that."

Tears threatened, and Lily fought to gulp them down. "Please, there must be something else I can do."

Fredericks gave her a hard look. "Listen up, Miss St. Claire, we're—"

"I'll settle her debts."

The three men looked past Lily to the back of the trade room. Lily whirled, her hopes soaring, searching the crowd for the man who'd made the offer.

North Walker stepped forward, sparing not even a glance at Lily.

"I'll trade you," he said to Fredericks. "For her."

Snickers rumbled from the men.

"Hmm…" Fredericks rubbed his chin thoughtfully. He glanced at Sykes, then at Becker.

"I guess we can hear him out," Fredericks said with a casual shrug.

"All right by me," Becker agreed.

North looked at Lily. "Go outside."

She couldn't move. She could barely think.

"Go outside," he told her again, more harshly this time.

Lily's temper flared. She'd had enough of men today—every single one of them. And she wanted to tell them all exactly what she thought of them, but decided it more prudent to keep her mouth shut for the moment.

She pushed her chin up, whirled and strode out of the room with all the dignity Madame DuBois had taught her, despite feeling the hot gaze of every man in the room on her back.

Outside, she eyed the gate and, for a moment, contemplated making a break for it. Right now with her anger up and her heart pounding, Lily thought she might actually hike all the way to Aunt Maribel's home in Richmond—by sundown.

That foolish notion left a moment later when Jacob Tanner squeezed through the crowd in the trade room and walked over to her.

Embarrassment heated her cheeks. Jacob was a nice young man, and he'd been present for her humiliation. He looked as uncomfortable as she when he stopped next to her.

"They had no right, saying those things and talking to you the way they did," Jacob said softly, nodding toward the trade room. "It ain't right, but… Well, that's the way it is around here."

Lily nodded, comforted and mollified somewhat by his compassionate words.

"Why do people stay here, Jacob?" she asked. "Why do you stay?"

He gazed thoughtfully across the plaza. "Came out here a couple of years ago with my ma and pa, my sister. We all got sick. They died."

"Oh, Jacob, that's so sad," Lily said, feeling a new kinship with him. "But why do you stay? Why don't you go back home?"

"Got no home to go back to," Jacob said with a shrug. "My pa sold our farm in Tennessee when he decided we needed to come out here."

"Don't you have any family back there?"

"Yes, some. But I haven't heard nothing from

them in so many years now—'' Jacob stopped abruptly as North walked out of the trade room. ''You take care now, Miss Lily,'' he said, and hurried away.

''They can't do this,'' Lily insisted to North, her anger flaring again. ''They can't force me to stay under those—conditions. Where is the sheriff of this territory?''

''*They're* the law around here,'' North told her and jerked his chin toward the trade room. ''They can do whatever they want.''

Her boiling anger cooled slightly because she knew he was right. Jacob had told her the same thing.

''Why are you helping me?'' she asked North. ''You heard what the other men said about me. I'm of no value to anyone here.''

He eased a little closer. ''I think you're perfect,'' he said softly.

Her anger dissolved and an odd tingling took its place, deep inside Lily.

Then his gaze dropped to the hem of her dress and rose slowly, deliberately over her waist, lingered on her bosom, and finally rested on her face.

''For what I have in mind for you, Miss St. Claire,'' he said, ''you're perfect.''

Chapter Five

She'd brought the fort to a complete standstill, it seemed.

An unnatural silence hung over the place as Lily crept through the alley and once more took her hiding place among the stacks of crates.

North had insisted she go to her quarters and remain there, but Lily had watched out the window and seen the men who had gathered in the trade room to witness her humiliation head toward the stable.

Now, every man in the fort, it seemed, stood in a loose circle, maintaining a discreet distance from Hiram Fredericks, Oliver Sykes, Sam Becker. And North, of course.

Once more, it seemed she was their entertainment.

With practiced ease, North dickered with the three men. Lily couldn't hear their words, but she could tell by the frowns, head shakes and shrugs that negotiations were underway.

For her.

What would North offer in trade for her? Lily wondered as she watched. That beautiful stallion she'd seen him with in the corral? An item of greater value? Did North possess something that Fredericks and the other men would find acceptable in her stead? For a moment she supposed a woman should be flattered by all this attention. Under other circumstances, that might be true.

Watching North, she thought once again that he was rescuing her, saving her from a terrible fate. But Lily couldn't work up any gratitude or compassion for him, not yet, anyway.

Not until she knew what he expected in return.

A murmur rose from the crowd gathered around the negotiators. Several of the men shook their heads—whether in amazement or dismay, Lily couldn't tell. North clasped hands with Fredericks, then Sykes and Becker.

So, it was done.

Lily's heart pounded a little harder as she watched North go into the corral, then disappear into the stable. The stallion. The finest example of horseflesh she'd seen at the fort—surely the most highly prized commodity in the territory. Is that what he'd traded? For her?

Then a snicker went through the crowd and sev-

eral men laughed aloud as North led three horses
from the stable, then out of the corral, and handed
the lead ropes over to Fredericks.

Humiliation burned Lily's cheeks like a hot
brand, stealing her breath. Three old nags. Sway-
back, heads hanging, hoofs dragging.

Worthless.

Which, apparently, was what North considered
her.

Some of the men seemed to think so, too, because
the chuckles continued.

"Hey, North," one man called, "I still think
you're getting the worse end of this bargain."

More laughter rose from the men as they drifted
away; they would be talking about this for days.

North shook hands once more with Fredericks,
Sykes and Becker. Apparently, they were pleased
with the deal, and for that, Lily knew she should be
grateful. Yet she'd never been so insulted in her life.

Three broken-down, worn-out horses? That's all
North had offered in trade for her? That's all he
believed she was worth?

When Becker led the horses back into the stable
and Fredericks and Sykes headed to the trade room,
Lily climbed down from the crates. She stomped
over to North and blocked his path.

"That's *it?*" she demanded, flinging her hand toward the stable.

North gazed at her, his brows pulled together.

"*That's* what you think I'm worth?" she asked, once more gesturing with her hand.

He leaned his head slightly sideways, just looking at her.

"I know you speak English!" Lily declared. She pulled herself up a little taller. "In polite society, a gentleman answers a question posed by a lady."

"This isn't exactly polite society," North told her. "And as you've already said, Miss St. Claire, I'm no gentleman."

"Are you suggesting that I should have no expectation of civility from you?" Lily demanded.

North just looked at her. "Are you still speaking English?"

"Of course I am!" Lily reined in her runaway temper. Alienating him would do her no good.

She turned their conversation to a more pressing issue, though she could barely bring it up without blushing.

"I—I'd like to know what you...expect of me," Lily said.

"I expect you to be what you are," North told her, as if it should be obvious. "A white woman. That's what I want. Now, pack your things. We're leaving."

"Leaving?" A cold chill swept up Lily's spine. She drew back from him. The fort that had been so foreign, so frightening to her now seemed as if it were the safest of havens.

"Do you think you can order me around because you've paid my debt?" Lily asked indignantly. "As if I'm your property?"

North expression hardened. "If this doesn't suit you, Miss St. Claire, I'm sure Fredericks is still willing to set you up in business."

Lily flushed but refused to look away. "All right," she admitted. "I do owe you for settling my debts. If you'll just let me leave, I'll go to my aunt's home in Richmond. She's very wealthy. She'll arrange to send you your money immediately."

"The only place you're going is with me," North told her. "And when I'm finished with you, I don't care where you go."

For a woman who'd talked nearly nonstop since the first time North had laid eyes on her, Lily hadn't spoken a word to him—or anyone else—since she'd climbed into the wagon and left the fort.

Whoever had stolen her horses and her belongings had damaged the wagon considerably; he didn't know for certain but strongly suspected the culprits were the three men who'd ridden into the fort with her, then taken off for Santa Fe the morning her father died.

North figured the thieves must have speculated—wrongly—that she would mount an effort to pursue them and recover her possessions, and damaging the wagon would prevent that.

He'd done minimal repairs and hitched up a team of his own horses to make the journey from the fort. Still, the wagon creaked and moaned with every turn of its wobbly wheels.

Lily sat huddled at the rear of the wagon, the torn canvas flapping in the breeze. He'd thought that she would sit up front beside him on the seat, but she hadn't. North wasn't sure why he'd expected her to, or why it bothered him that she hadn't.

He wasn't sure why many things about Lily troubled him.

Like the way she smelled. Fresh and clean. Flowers in a spring meadow after a rain shower. No other woman he'd ever known had smelled that way.

North shifted on the seat, the unexpected tingling of desire startling him. Desire for Lily, of all women.

Determinedly, he pushed her from his thoughts. More pressing issues needed his time, his thoughts and certainly his energy. He didn't want to think about her.

Or about what awaited them both at the end of the day.

North hoped he wasn't making the biggest mistake of his life.

Each moment that passed took Lily farther and farther away from the fort, away from civilization…such as it was, anyway.

Seated at the rear of the wagon, her back to North, she watched the scenery roll away. Bent's Fort had disappeared from view long ago; she'd trained her gaze on it until the very last second. Now she searched the landscape for other identifying markers: outcroppings of rocks, a unique stand of cottonwoods, an oddly shaped ditch or rise, anything that might lead her back to the fort—if she managed to escape from wherever North was taking her.

A knot drew tighter in her stomach. She had no idea how long they might travel, when they might stop, or where they were headed.

Yet she feared she knew what would happen when they arrived.

He'd hold her captive. Ravish her. Surely, he would. Why else would he want her?

For a moment, Lily wondered if she'd have been better off remaining at the fort. If she'd actually been set up in business as a prostitute, as Hiram Fredericks and the other men had wanted, at least she'd have an accounting of her debt. If North demanded the same sort of repayment, how would she keep track? She had no idea how much to charge. Would she have to remain his captive until he decided her debt was paid?

Her head spun slightly and her stomach ached. Among the few items the robbers hadn't taken from her wagon was a quilt, and Lily was tempted to curl up on it and sleep. But she didn't dare. She had to remain vigilant. Had to keep watch. Memorize the trail back to the fort. Look for an opportunity to escape.

Glumly, she gazed at the scenery. They hadn't passed a house, cabin, tent or another human being since leaving the fort.

She'd never see Aunt Maribel again.

Gradually, the prairie blended into trees and a discernable trail was evident through the forest. Another wave of anxiety washed through Lily. Did that mean a settlement was up ahead? Or was he taking her to the Cheyenne village?

White women never escaped an Indian village. Everyone on the wagon train had said so.

To her surprise, the wagon pulled to a stop in front of a small log cabin, sheltered beneath the bows of towering trees. Several outbuildings and a modest barn stood a short distance away, along with a corral holding a number of horses.

Lily leaned sideways, glimpsing the place through the tears in the canvas.

"Where are we?" she asked, both curious and frightened.

"We're home." North jumped down from the seat. "My home."

Lily gulped hard. "This—this is where we're... staying?"

Fear almost caused her to double over. Nothing

around for miles. No one to hear her screams. Not a soul, probably, who even knew she was here.

"Let's go," North called, and waved her toward the cabin.

Lily folded her arms tight across her middle and rocked forward. She couldn't get up. She simply could not.

He walked back to the end of the wagon and gazed up at her. "What's wrong?"

Lily couldn't give him an answer. Where would she begin? She caught the edge of the quilt and pulled it onto her lap.

"Are you sick?" North lowered the tailgate.

Of course she was sick. Sick with worry and fear. Lily gulped down the lump of emotion that rose into her throat. She couldn't stand. Her legs wouldn't hold her up.

Lily glanced at North. He stood at the tailgate gazing up at her, concern in his expression.

He had his nerve, she decided suddenly. Inquiring about her health and looking concerned—after he'd traded three horses for her and brought her here as if she were so much livestock.

She wouldn't go peaceably. The notion struck Lily like a bolt of lightning, charging her with strength. She wouldn't bend to his will, allow him to do anything he chose. She wouldn't.

With a quick snap, Lily unfurled the quilt and threw it over North's head. She leaped to the ground, shouldered him in the chest with all the strength she could muster—enough to knock him back a step—and raced down the trail.

Lily hiked up her dress, desperate to get away. She'd bought herself a few seconds. Would it be enough? It had to be.

Footsteps pounded behind her. Lily glanced back. North. She screamed and ran harder. An arm looped her stomach and jerked her off her feet, stealing her breath away.

"Let me go!" Lily kicked, banged away at him with her elbows. His arm was like a steel band around her middle, but she wiggled furiously until she broke free. She ran again. He caught her again, this time jerking her backward by her arm.

Lily's ankle twisted. She pitched forward. North lurched toward her. Their feet tangled. They both went down.

She landed atop him, her face inches from his. Her breasts molded against his hard chest. Her thighs lay against his. Stunned, they both stilled, gazing into each other eyes.

Heat rose from him, saturating her through the layers of their clothing. His breath, hot and thick, puffed against her chin. A long, endless moment passed. Lily couldn't move. Held captive by nothing more than his gaze, she lay there.

He shifted beneath her and she gasped as the hard length of him dug into her thigh. Lily scrambled to her feet, and ran. She dashed through the forest, weaving through trees, leaping exposed roots, vines and shrubs.

North caught her again, once more looping his arm around her waist. He jerked her off her feet. Lily twisted, struggling desperately until she escaped his grasp again. But before she could run, he grabbed her wrist. Lily spun away yet he held her firmly, his strong fingers digging into her flesh.

"Where the hell do you think you're going?" he demanded, waving his other hand to encompass the forest around them.

"Let me go!" She pulled against him. "Please! Let me go!"

"You'll die out there by yourself!" North declared. "What's the matter with you?"

Tears, fright, horror, every ragged emotion that tore through Lily boiled down to one: anger. She balled up her fist and pounded his chest.

North fended off her blows, more a nuisance than a threat, then leaned forward and heaved her over his shoulder.

"No!" She pounded her fists against his back. He jolted her, driving his shoulder into her stomach, taking away her breath. The world whirled as he turned and carried her toward the cabin.

He opened the door, stepped inside and dumped her to the floor.

Stunned, Lily lay there gasping for breath. A lock

of her hair hung over her eyes, her sleeve was torn, her body ached. North towered over her.

"You—you animal!" she cried.

"Who's she?"

Lily turned at the sound of another voice. A young girl, probably no older than fifteen, stood at the table. Golden braids hung past her shoulders.

Lily pushed herself up, bracing her arms behind her. She looked at the girl, then North.

"You beast! You've captured another girl, as well, for your filthy pleasure!"

North frowned. "She's my sister."

"Your *sister?*" Lily's lips turned down with revulsion. "You really *are* a perverted beast!"

"What's she doing here?" the young girl asked, walking closer.

North grumbled, batting at his trousers to brush away the dirt. "I brought her for you."

The girl drew back slightly, regarding Lily with suspicion. "What for?"

"She's going to teach you to be a lady."

Chapter Six

"What?" the girl exclaimed, frowning and stepping closer.

"You heard me," North told her. "She's going to teach you to be a lady."

The girl turned her gaze on Lily once more. Still seated on the floor, Lily stared right back. She couldn't help herself.

The girl was beautiful. Pale-white skin, golden-blond hair. Yet she had brown eyes—dark and liquid, the same as North's. She could easily have been taken for white, were it not for the doeskin dress and colorfully beaded moccasins she wore.

Contempt turned the corners of the girl's lips down as she assessed Lily. Then, without a word and only a contemptuous look at North, she darted past him and ran out of the cabin. He turned, and Lily thought for a moment that he would go after her, but instead he swung around to Lily again.

North pointed his finger at her. "Don't you ever hit me again."

He didn't shout, didn't even speak loudly, but the venom in his tone caused Lily to shrink back from him. She cast about the cabin, looking for an escape.

The rough-hewn log house was one room. A bunk piled with buffalo robes stood in the far corner. A stone fireplace took up nearly an entire wall. The rest of the cabin held a table and chairs, a stove, shelves. It was functional, spartan, but clean.

And there was no way out, Lily saw, except for the doorway that, certainly, North had no intention of letting her use.

She sat on the floor for a moment expecting North to offer his assistance in her getting to her feet. When he didn't, she got up on her own. They eyed each other warily as she tucked an errant lock of hair behind her ear and brushed at the dirt on her dress.

"Is that really the reason you brought me here?" Lily wanted to know, gesturing out the door in the general direction his sister had run. "For your sister? For me to teach her?"

North's brows pulled together. He looked offended. "I wouldn't lie."

Lily didn't respond right away and that seemed to insult him further.

"Do you think I would lie?" he demanded.

"It's just that," she said, threading her fingers

together in front of her, "well, I've heard so many stories of Indians who capture white women and—"

"And what?"

Lily flushed, unable to bring herself to say the words aloud. She made a little spinning gesture with her hand. "And…"

North copied her actions, waving his hands along with her. "And?"

She fought off her embarrassment. "They capture white women and—and they force them to have… relations…with them."

His brows drew together. She was sure that he really didn't understand the word. "Relations?"

Lily huffed. "Yes, relations. *Relations.* Intimate acts. Private moments. Procreation. A man and a woman—*together.*"

"Oh." North nodded his head, understanding finally dawning on him, apparently. Then his frown returned and he looked Lily up and down. "You think that's why I brought you here?"

He'd asked as if it were the most outlandish thing he'd ever imagined.

"Well, it isn't unheard of," Lily murmured, trying hard not to let her discomfort with the situation show. Good gracious, the problems she'd confronted and the things she'd had to discuss lately. Madame DuBois had covered none of this in any of her classes.

North pressed his fingers against his chin and drew his head back slightly, looking her up and down. With a critical eye, his gaze roamed her from head to foot, as if he were evaluating a horse for trade.

''I have no such want for you.'' He shook his head. ''You'll see that I don't.''

She should have been relieved, yet she wasn't. The man claimed that he intended no ill will toward her, and implied that she should trust him.

But how could she? She'd met him only recently. She didn't know him—really know him. Certainly not well enough to decide whether or not he was either truthful or trustworthy.

Her own father had deceived her. Lily's stomach ached at the memory. He'd kept things from her. He'd deliberately lied to her. He'd allowed her to accompany him on this trip west, all the while knowing full well that it might be a financial failure, that her future, her well-being could be put at risk.

The men at the fort had been just as deceitful. They'd pretended to be her friends, to help her in her time of need, all the while keeping a tally of their every good deed, running up her tab. Then they'd tried to bully her into a disgusting job—for their own gain.

Gazing at North, Lily hardened her heart. She wouldn't trust him, no matter what he said.

"You're to teach my sister to be a lady. Starting right now." North spun and headed out the door.

"No."

He stopped. Slowly, he turned, his expression grim, almost daring her to speak again.

Lily pushed her chin up slightly. She didn't trust him and she certainly wouldn't cooperate with him.

"I won't do it," she told him.

North stepped closer. "Yes, you will."

"I won't. I don't like it here. I don't want to be here. I won't stay." Lily flung out both arms. "You can't watch me every second of the day and night. I'll escape and make my way east, somehow."

The anger left North's face, crowded out by concern. "Don't, Lily. Don't try it. Don't even think it. You won't last two days in the wilderness alone."

"I want to go home," Lily told him, unable to fend off the sudden rush of emotion.

"I need you here to teach my sister."

"No."

"It's important."

Lily shook her head. "Not to me."

"I settled your debts."

"I didn't ask you to do that."

"You're obligated to me," he told her.

"You may as well let me go now, because I won't do anything to help you," she vowed, and she'd never meant anything more in her entire life. "There's nothing you can do to change my mind."

Lily fought to hold back a wave of tears and willed herself to be strong. She wouldn't cooperate with him, wouldn't do anything he wanted, not now, not in a hundred years.

North seemed to read the determination on her face. He took a breath, let it out slowly.

"Change is coming to the land," he said softly. "White settlers will continue westward, encroaching on the Indians. The government with its laws will follow. There are skirmishes among the whites and Indians. Attacks. Killings. There is fear, distrust, misunderstanding and hostility on both sides."

"What does any of that have to do with me?" Lily asked impatiently.

"No good will come from fighting. Many will die, both whites and Indians. If we are to live side by side on the land, there must be understanding between the two peoples," North said. "I want my sister to travel to the East, to talk to government officials, to give lectures, to help everyone understand the ways of the Indians."

A few moments passed while Lily contemplated what he'd said.

"And you want me to teach her proper manners for Eastern society?" she asked.

"You saw what she looks like," North said, nodding outside.

"She's beautiful," Lily said. "She looks white. She must favor your father."

"Her appearance will help make her acceptable in the East, but she must know the customs if she is to be fully accepted," North said. "So you see, it's very important that you stay and help her. There is no one else who can teach my sister but you."

Lily couldn't deny that North's idea was a good one. She knew the fear most people in the East had of the Indians. On the wagon train, there was much talk about possible uprisings and attacks, stories of what Indians were capable of doing.

Settlers were coming west in greater numbers all the time. Indians and white alike were in peril.

Yet standing in the one-room cabin, in the middle of the wilderness, thousands of miles from home and family, unsure of what was to become of her, Lily couldn't bring herself to care.

"You'll have to find someone else," she said. "I won't help you."

"There is no one else."

Lily shrugged. "This isn't my problem."

"It's everyone's problem," North insisted.

"No." Lily turned away, suddenly tired and weary. Tears threatened once again. She couldn't solve the world's problems—shouldn't be expected to.

Because at the moment, she couldn't even solve her own problems.

"I'll take you home," North said.

Lily stilled, not sure she'd heard him correctly.

She swung around and brushed the tears from her face with the backs of her hands.

"What did you say?" she asked softly.

"If you teach my sister," North said, "I'll take you home."

"To my aunt's house?" she asked, quickly. "It's in Virginia. That's a long way—"

"I know where Virginia is."

"And you'll take me there?" she asked, almost afraid to say the words aloud.

"I'll fix your wagon, load it with supplies, and escort you to her front door," North said.

"You'd do that?" A glimmer of hope—the only one she'd experienced in weeks—sparked inside Lily. "You'd really do that?"

"Teach my sister," North said, "and I will deliver you safely to your aunt's home."

"And all I have to do is teach your sister to be a lady?" Lily asked. "That's it?"

North nodded. "That's it."

"Do you promise?"

He looked a little irritated that she'd questioned his honesty, but said, "You have my word of honor. My solemn oath."

Only a moment ago, she'd decided that she couldn't trust North. Did she believe him now? His promise to take her to Virginia would require a massive undertaking—months on the Trail, then overland to Virginia. Expensive provisions, hardship.

Lily searched his face, looking for some clue, some hint of his honesty. She saw nothing that swayed her. Nothing that made her believe—or disbelieve—that he would do as he promised.

So where did that leave her? Stranded in the wilderness with no hope of ever getting to civilization again.

Unless North kept his word.

At the moment, he was her only option.

Lily nodded slowly. "All right, then, I'll help you. I'll teach your sister."

He looked hard at her. "And do I have your solemn oath?"

Apparently, North didn't trust her completely, either. She couldn't blame him.

"Yes," Lily assured him.

"You won't try to run away the minute my back is turned?"

"I have no reason to." Lily's gaze locked with his. "As long as you keep your word."

They looked at each other, a fragile, thin bond of trust stretching between them.

Another moment passed in silence, then Lily said, "The quicker I train your sister, the quicker I can go home. So, let's get started."

She looked past him out the door, anxious to begin her new task. "Is your sister still here? She didn't leave, did she?"

North stepped to the door and shouted, "Hannah!"

"An English name," Lily realized, more than a little surprised.

"To satisfy our father," North explained, still gazing out the door.

"Does she have a Cheyenne name?"

"Little Moon."

"That's lovely," Lily said, still looking past him out the door. "Does she live with you?"

"Sometimes here, and at other times at the village." He nodded through the forest.

"What about you?" she asked. "Do you have a Cheyenne name, also?"

"Nomeohtse," he said, and glanced back at her. "It means Going with the Wind."

Lily watched anxiously, and finally North's sister emerged from the trees near the barn. Hannah. Little Moon. Her ticket home.

Quickly, a regimen of deportment and etiquette training flashed in Lily's mind. She'd attended such classes since she was only a child. She'd been taught by the finest instructors available. No one—absolutely no one—was better prepared to teach this girl than Lily.

Her stomach fluttered with delight. Because as soon as she was finished, she could go home.

As long as North kept his word.

Home. Aunt Maribel. Gentlemen. Gracious ladies. Hot baths. Lovely gowns. Civilization.

North stepped aside as Hannah walked into the cabin. She lurked near the door, and gave Lily a suspicious look.

Lily was tempted to throw both arms around the young girl and squeeze her tight in a giant hug, but thought better of it.

Instead she said, "Hannah, I'm Miss Lily St. Claire, of Saint Louis. You have no idea how truly pleased I am to meet you."

Hannah frowned up at her brother, still unhappy, silently asking for an explanation.

"You're going to the East," North said. "You have to learn manners."

"But I don't want to go to the East," she replied, shaking her head.

North jerked his chin toward Lily. "She will teach you what you need to know."

Hannah looked at Lily with newfound contempt. She backed away.

"I don't want to learn manners," she said.

North frowned. "Listen, Hannah, you will—"

"No! I'm not going, and nothing you can say will change my mind!"

Hannah raced out of the cabin.

Chapter Seven

"Well, then, I guess that settles everything," Lily declared, raising her palms in resignation, "I'll just leave."

North frowned down at her.

Lily gestured toward Hannah as she disappeared into the woods. "Your sister has no desire to learn manners. She said so quite plainly. That means there's no reason for me to stay. Let's get to the wagon. If we hurry, we can make it to the fort before dark."

North shifted in front of her, blocking the doorway. "You're not going anywhere."

"But your sister—"

"—will do as she's told," North said. His frown deepened. "And you're not going to leave. You gave your word."

Yes, she had, but now the circumstances were different—thankfully.

"I can't teach an unwilling pupil," Lily pointed out. "It's impossible. Believe me, I know. I've seen this sort of thing happen before with some of the other students in the schools I attended."

"Then you'd better figure out a way to make her want to learn, because you're not going home until she does." North stalked out the door.

"But…" Lily's shoulders sagged as she watched him walk away. She considered going after him, stating her case once more, arguing her cause for returning home immediately, but doubted it would do any good. He'd looked and sounded determined.

With a heavy sigh, Lily stood in the doorway gazing outside. This long day had taken a physical and emotional toll on her. Various aches and pains reminded Lily of the escape attempt she'd made and the ensuing wrestling match with North.

A strange tingle warmed her stomach. He was so strong. He'd scooped her up with one arm. He could have hurt her—easily—if he'd wanted to. Then she'd fallen on top of him. Lily flushed, recalling his hard body beneath hers, the heat he'd given off, the way the curves of her body had molded against his.

She pushed the memory away. Good gracious, what would Madame DuBois think? Proper young women simply did not have such thoughts.

More pressing matters required her brain power, Lily decided. She should be focusing on them. But, at the moment, she was simply too tired and too hungry to contemplate them.

Through the thick forest, the glowing orange sun hovered just above the horizon, bringing the day to a close. It would be dark soon. Lily had to find something to eat, and her belongings had to be brought into the cabin. She'd have to make herself comfortable here, somehow, since it seemed she was marooned here indefinitely.

North had disappeared into the barn and no one else was around to help carry her things in from the wagon. She'd have to do it herself. She was in no mood to ask North for his help, anyway.

At the rear of the wagon, Lily hiked up her skirt and climbed inside. With considerable effort, she scooted the satchels and her heavy trunks onto the tailgate, then jumped to the ground, her dress and petticoats billowing out around her.

Lily smoothed down her skirt. Oh, yes, such a lady. If Madame DuBois saw her right now the woman would surely faint dead away.

She carried the satchels into the cabin and dropped them in the corner near the bunk. When she stepped outside again, she found North there, tending the horses.

"My trunks need to be unloaded," Lily said.

He glanced back at her, but didn't say anything. Nor did he stop what he was doing to help her.

Lily gave him another moment, and when he still

didn't move, she huffed irritably and stomped to the rear of the wagon.

She caught one of the trunks by its handles and pulled it down. Its weight was too much. She staggered back, then let it drop to the ground.

The loose lock of her hair fell forward again. She stuck it behind her ear, planted her fists on her hips, and contemplated the trunk. Too heavy to carry, she'd have to drag or push it inside.

"I'd just like to point out," Lily called to North, "that women in the East don't do this sort of thing. They don't carry their own trunks."

He paused and looked back at her.

"In the East, gentlemen do it for them," she said pointedly.

North walked to the rear of the wagon. "Indian women do their own work. Nobody helps them."

"Do I look like an Indian woman to you?" Lily demanded. She stretched out both arms, presenting herself. "Does anything about me—anything at all—cause you to mistake me for an Indian?"

North looked at her, and took his time in doing so. Head to toe, he assessed her. Heat seemed to arc from him to her, suddenly warming Lily.

His raised his eyebrow. "I assure you, Miss St. Claire, absolutely nothing about you reminds me of the hardworking women of my village."

She put her arms down, trying to fight off the odd

feelings coursing through her, and the sting of his veiled insult.

"Then do you suppose you could carry these trunks into the cabin for me?" she asked.

He didn't answer, nor did he make a move to lift the trunk for her.

"Oh, never mind." Lily butted in front of him. "Granted, my talents don't include lifting and hauling. But, I assure you, in my own circle, I'm worth quite a bit—certainly more than those three old nags you traded to Hiram Fredericks."

"The deal suited Fredericks."

"I don't see why."

"Because he knew you'd always be too much trouble." North stepped in front of her, picked up the trunk and carried it into the cabin.

The urge to shout a retort at his broad back nearly overcame Lily, but she held her tongue.

After North had moved all her belongings into the cabin, he led the team to the barn while Lily stared at her trunks and satchels. She should unpack. Get her things in order. She certainly couldn't go about her daily routine under these conditions.

Yet part of her held back. By some miracle, might North let her leave? It could happen. Couldn't it?

Not likely, she realized, coming to her senses. Still, she couldn't bring herself to unpack and—even remotely—think of this place as home.

Later, North came back into the cabin, heated

beans and meat on the stove and sat down at the table to eat. He hadn't asked Lily for her assistance, but he'd made enough for them both. She scooped a little food onto the tin plate and sat down at the other end of the table, as far away from him as she could.

Darkness had fallen and he'd lit a lantern in the center of the table. Lily picked up her spoon, fiddled with it for a moment, then glanced outside.

"Isn't Hannah coming back?" she asked.

North shrugged.

"Is she all right?" Lily asked, glancing outside once again. "Do you think something happened to her? It's dark and—"

"Hannah can take care of herself," North said. "She's gone to the village."

"Oh…"

Lily tasted the beans. Earlier, she'd tried to talk North out of keeping her here and he'd refused to even consider the possibility. She decided it was worth another try.

"It will be impossible for me to teach your sister, if she's not willing to learn," Lily said. "Surely you can see that."

North glanced up from his plate. "Nothing is impossible."

"How can I teach her if she isn't even here?" Lily asked, gesturing to the two unoccupied chairs at the table, trying to sound reasonable and not scream at him.

He glared at her, then resumed eating.

"Do you expect me to traipse through the woods and find her?" Lily asked. "Perhaps explain the proper seating arrangement for a formal supper as I'm dragging her back to the cabin?"

He looked slightly annoyed, but said, "I'll bring her here."

"Did you explain to her what this is all about?" Lily asked. "Before I got here, did you tell her about your plan?"

"No."

"No?" Lily gasped. "You just sprang it on her today? With no preparation? No explanation? And you expected her to simply go along with the idea of leaving her home, her family, all the things—"

North slapped his spoon down on the table. "If all Eastern women talk this much at mealtime, don't teach *that* to Hannah."

He pushed up from the table, gathered their plates and made quick work of washing them in the bucket beside the stove. Lily almost offered to help, but he didn't look as if he needed any, and she didn't want to ask where to find a towel and where everything belonged. Yet another demonstration of her incompetence held no appeal so late in this long day.

When he'd finished the dishes, North moved the lantern from the table to the shelf beside the bunk.

He sorted through the buffalo robes, selected three and dropped them on the floor.

"You can use these," he said.

Lily kept her distance. "For what?"

"Sleeping."

"Sleep—"

Lily drew in a quick breath as North sat on the edge of the bunk, pulled off his boots and socks, then rose and dropped his suspenders.

"What—what are you doing?" she gasped.

"Going to bed," he said, opening his cuffs and unfastening his shirt buttons.

"But you can't—"

He pulled off his shirt. Beneath it, the white cotton of his long johns shone brightly in the dim lantern light. North reached for the top button of his trousers.

"Stop!" Lily rushed forward and clamped her hands over his.

Startled, North looked down at their hands locked together. He lifted his gaze to her face.

Lily gulped and backed away, her fingers burning. "You mustn't...undress."

"Eastern men sleep with their clothes on?" he asked.

"No, it's just that—"

Lily tried to keep her gaze on the floor, the wall, the ceiling—anywhere but on North. Yet her mutinous eyes kept turning his way.

Even without his shoes on, he was tall—and his feet were huge. The snug fit of his underwear emphasized the width of his shoulders, the broadness of his chest, the hard edges of the muscles across his trim belly.

Heat surged through Lily, causing her heart to beat faster. Could North feel her warmth? Surely he could hear the pounding of her heart.

Lily forced down her surging emotions and determinedly turned her gaze onto his face, fighting off the desire to glance once more at his chest.

"It's inappropriate for a man and a woman to… sleep…in the same room. Unless they're married, of course," she explained. "So you'll have to sleep outside, or in the barn."

His brow rose. "*I'll* have to sleep outside or in the barn?"

Her embarrassment evaporated, replaced by indignation. "You don't think *I* should sleep outside, do you?"

North looked at her as if he did, in fact, see nothing wrong with it.

Lily straightened her shoulders. "You wanted a white woman. So here I am. And I am not in the habit of sleeping out of doors or in barns."

North gave her a long, hard look.

For a moment, Lily feared he'd refuse to leave. That he'd insist that she, in fact, sleep outside.

Finally, North yanked up his boots and socks,

grabbed two buffalo robes and stalked to the door. He looked back at her.

"Are there *any* Eastern customs favorable to men? Any at all?"

He looked frustrated and, somehow, oddly comical. Lily resisted the urge to smile. "No. Not really."

North stalked out of the cabin, slamming the door behind him.

"Fine thing," he grumbled, "a man being thrown out of his own home."

The grass was soft and cool beneath his bare feet as he headed toward the barn. Overhead, the slice of moon offered meager light.

The thought occurred to him that he should have made Lily sleep in the barn. But he doubted she'd have stayed there all night. Surely, she'd have come back inside and awakened him over and over again, wanting to talk about something.

The wooden barn door creaked as North opened it. A row of stalls that led into the corral was off to his right. On the left were stores of feed, supplies and tack.

North dropped his robes and boots into the stall closest to the door. He turned and gazed at the cabin. His cabin. The cabin in which he should be sleeping.

White women. His father had often spoken of his family in the East, but he'd never mentioned that the women were this helpless, this much trouble. If

North had known, he might not have gone through with this plan of his.

But even as he thought those words, he couldn't imagine Lily not being in his cabin, with him here at his home. After so short a time, it already felt as if she belonged here.

There was something about her...

Standing in the silence of the cool night, North rested his shoulder against the door. Maybe it was her eyes. Blue. Bright blue, at times. Somehow they seemed to darken when she was angry. He'd never seen blue eyes on a woman before.

A familiar—and not unpleasant—stirring caught North by surprise, just as it had on the journey to the cabin today. A physical desire he hadn't expected.

Visions of what Lily might be doing at this very moment flashed in his mind.

What did women like her sleep in? A soft, delicate garment similar to the dresses she wore?

Or would she sleep naked?

The mental image of Lily's white skin gleaming in the lantern light caused North's condition to worsen with unexpected force.

He gritted his teeth and turned away from the cabin. Hannah had better learn Eastern ways—and quick.

Chapter Eight

Lily awoke with a start. A noise. She'd heard a noise.

Fighting off the urge to leap to her feet, Lily huddled deeper beneath the buffalo robes. Her ears strained, searching the still night silence for the sound, waiting for it to come again. A full minute ticked by, then another. Nothing.

But she'd heard something. Something outside the cabin. She was sure of it.

An animal, perhaps? A bear? A more vicious predator hunting for food?

An intruder. Lily gasped in the silent cabin. An outlaw or an army deserter? Renegade Indians?

Or was it North?

Lily pushed herself up on her elbow. He'd said he had no interest in her beyond the need for her teaching skills. He'd acted as if the idea that there was anything more were ridiculous.

Had he changed his mind?

Or was it all a ruse?

Lily cringed, chastising herself for believing him—even for a moment. She should never have trusted him. Hadn't she seen enough deceitful men on this journey to convince her?

She squinted at the door across the room. Closed tight, still.

Could she have been wrong to suspect North? No, she decided, not entirely.

Lily relaxed onto the bunk again. Perhaps she was mistaken and hadn't heard a sound at all. Perhaps she'd been dreaming and—

The noise again. Lily threw back the robes and crept to the open window. The cool breeze blew through the thin fabric of her yellow nightgown, chilling her. She dropped to her knees, pushed her dark hair over her shoulder, and peeked out.

Faint moonlight illuminated the barn and corral, the other outbuildings. Nothing seemed amiss as she watched, and just as she was doubting herself again, a figure separated itself from the shadow of the barn.

North.

Lily pressed her fingers to her lips to seal in her surprised gasp. His dark suspenders and trousers, his gleaming black hair contrasted against the white fabric of his long johns.

Panic spread through her. It was the middle of the night. Why would he be up and about unless—

He was coming after her.

Lily's gaze darted about the cabin, looking for a weapon of some sort, readying herself to fight him off. She glanced outside again. Another man stepped into the moonlight.

Her fear of North dissolved. Lily sank lower in front of the window, drew her arms closer, trying to make herself as small as possible, some instinct warning her to keep watch, be ready to run.

The distance was too great for her to make out the man's face, yet something about him seemed familiar, jarred her memory. Tall, thin, a fringe of blond hair hanging from under his slouch hat.

Was it the man to whom North had given a packet of papers near the stable at Bent's Fort? She thought so, but couldn't be sure.

Lily watched as North and the man stood together. She guessed they were talking, but couldn't hear even a hum of conversation. Then, abruptly, the stranger strode away into the woods. North remained where he was, he too, watching the man. Several more moments passed, then he went back into the barn.

Lily remained crouched beneath the window watching the barn door. Minutes dragged by. She shivered in the breeze. When the door didn't open again and she saw no sign that North was approaching the cabin, she hurried to the bunk and slipped beneath the robes.

Of course, there could have been a dozen reasons a man would come to the cabin in the wee hours of the night and talk to North, but Lily couldn't think of a single one that made sense. She snuggled deeper beneath the robes and fell asleep.

When she woke again, once more in the darkness, sleep's hold allowed her to barely open her eyes. Vaguely she was aware of movement in the cabin. Then North came to stand over her.

"Shh," he whispered. "Don't be frightened."

Lily gasped and came fully awake. She scrambled backward on the bunk until she bumped the wall, desperate to get as far from North as she could.

He knelt beside the bunk. "There's nothing to fear. I won't hurt you."

The soft, gentle tone of his voice calmed her. She waved her hand toward the window. "I saw a man. Who was he?"

North shook his head. "There's no one here."

"Last night."

"A dream." North reached out his hand. For some reason, Lily didn't pull away. She allowed him to press his palm against her cheek. "No one has been here. It was a dream."

Gently, his fingers stroked her jaw. Lily relaxed onto the pillow once more.

North leaned closer. "Sleep now," he murmured,

his breath warm against her cheek. He pulled the buffalo robe higher on her shoulder.

Lily closed her eyes and drifted off to sleep.

At dawn, Lily woke to an odd feeling of comfort. North came to her mind immediately. She pushed back the robes and took in the cabin. No sign of him.

Yet he'd been here, hadn't he?

For a moment, Lily lay on the bunk, trying to recall the details of the night. North had been in the cabin, she decided. He'd been at her side, knelt beside the bunk. He'd touched her cheek.

Lily's hand went instinctively to the spot where his hand had stroked her face. How unseemly. A man intruding on her during the night while she was sleeping and wearing nothing but her nightgown. He'd promised he'd leave her alone, yet he hadn't.

Of course, he hadn't harmed her. He'd done nothing more than touch her cheek. Still…

And what about the other man? The one she'd seen at the barn with North?

Lily pushed the robes off and sat up. She'd seen him. She was certain of it. Yet North had told her it was a dream.

Lily got to her feet. She'd certainly ask him about it again.

The morning chill urged Lily to wash and dress quickly. As she did, she glanced out the window expecting to catch sight of North going about his chores and tending to the horses. Instead, she spotted Hannah.

The young woman stepped out of the woods, her golden hair reflecting the rays of the rising sun. She wore a doeskin dress and moccasins, both decorated with colorful beads. Like North, she moved as if she were part of the land, comfortable, at home here.

Lily couldn't imagine why North had thought his sister would ever leave this place.

The cabin door opened and Hannah stepped inside, her expression cold and determined.

"I am *not* going to be taught by you," she declared, flinging the words at Lily, as if they were an openhanded slap.

Lily was in no mood for a confrontation. Especially since she agreed with Hannah.

"That's perfectly all right with me," Lily told her.

Hannah took a step closer. "I'm not going to learn Eastern customs or manners."

"I don't think you should."

"And I am not leaving my home," Hannah said, drawing herself up taller and squaring her shoulders.

How much this young woman looked like North, Lily realized. The tilt of their heads, the jutting of their jaws. Both stubborn. Surely, the two of them argued most of the time.

"Has North explained this plan of his to you yet?" Lily asked.

"Yes. Over and over." Hannah rolled her eyes. "But I want nothing to do with it."

Lily folded her hands in front of her. "I completely agree with you. I think North's idea is silly, and he shouldn't expect you to be a part of it. It's unreasonable of him."

That seemed to take some of the fight out of Hannah. She relaxed her stance.

"In fact," Lily went on, warming to her subject, "I told your brother that there was nothing I could do here. I told him several times, actually."

"You did?" Hannah asked, looking surprised.

"Certainly. I offered to leave, but he wouldn't hear of it." Lily gestured in the direction of the barn. "Ask him yourself."

"North's gone."

A little chill ran up Lily's spine. She leaned around Hannah to see out the door, then glanced through the window. Was that why North was in the cabin before dawn? Because he was preparing to leave?

"Where did he go?" Lily asked, a feeling of fear and isolation coming over her unexpectedly.

Hannah shrugged as if she didn't know and didn't care, and walked to the cupboard. She pulled out a frying pan and placed it on the stove.

"When is he coming back?" Lily asked.

"I don't know," Hannah said, as she sorted

through the food supplies on the shelves beside the stove.

An ember of hope sparked inside Lily. Dare she try to escape, even though she'd given North her word that she wouldn't?

"North will be gone all day?" Lily asked.

"He told me to take care of you," Hannah said, with a glance back over her shoulder.

"Do you know the way to Bent's Fort?" Lily asked, trying to sound casual.

"He also told me that you might try to leave," Hannah said.

So, he didn't trust her, after all. He'd warned his sister to be on guard. Lily was slightly peeved that North hadn't counted on her to keep her word— even though, in fact, she hadn't intended to.

"But if you don't want me here," Lily said, walking closer, "and I don't want to be here, we could end this now if you'd help me get back to the fort. I could wait there until a wagon train came through heading east. I'm sure some good-hearted travelers would allow me to ride with them. I'm sure it's been done before."

Hannah turned back to the stove without answering. Lily's hopes sank. She'd get no help from Hannah. Apparently, she didn't agree with North, yet she wasn't willing to openly defy him.

While Hannah cooked their breakfast, Lily prepared the table. Aside from tin plates and cups, there was little available in the cabin to properly set a table. Hannah didn't seem to notice the distinct lack of amenities as she filled the plates with potatoes and eggs and they both sat down.

"North's idea isn't silly," Hannah said after a short while.

A few seconds passed before Lily recalled that she'd made that remark earlier. Hannah hadn't taken exception to it then, and it surprised Lily that she did so now.

"It's a good idea that someone should go to the East and teach everyone about the Indians," Hannah went on. "More and more settlers are coming here. They don't understand us. They don't understand how we live."

"They should stay home," Lily said, a bitterness creeping into her tone.

"You came," Hannah pointed out.

"I didn't understand what I was getting into." Lily shook her head. "If I'd known how hard it would be, or how it would turn out…"

"Perhaps *you* should tell the Easterners to stay away," Hannah suggested.

It wasn't a bad idea, Lily realized. But the Eastern newspapers were full of articles about riches in the West, and the glorious adventures of explorers. Politicians pushed for Western expansion. Settlers clamored for open land and new opportunities. Lily doubted her tale of hardship would deter many people; they'd already heard many terrible stories, anyway.

"My father died making the trip," Lily said, toying with her fork. "He and many others before him. I don't think anything can stop men and families from coming west. Unless the government steps in, of course."

"North says the men at the fort don't want the government involved out here," Hannah said. "Now, they're free to do as they please, with no one to stop them. They don't want that to change."

Anger coiled deep in Lily's stomach as she recalled the callous way Hiram Fredericks and his cronies had treated her at the fort. Charging her exorbitant fees, forbidding her to leave, attempting to hold her captive and force her into prostitution.

Hannah was right. The men at the fort did as they chose. They controlled trade, commerce, prices, availability of goods. And there was no one—certainly not a government presence—to stop them. The U.S. Army patrolled the area, but they had no authority to enforce laws. The Territory was wide open.

A deep sense of foreboding came over Lily. If she'd refused to go along with Fredericks's intention to set her up as a prostitute, if North hadn't stepped in and settled her debts, what might those men have done with her? And who would have stopped them? Who would have made them accountable?

"Perhaps I should do just that," Lily said, warming to the idea. "Perhaps I should tell everyone in the East exactly what's happening here. That would show those men at the fort."

"They'd kill you."

Lily gasped.

"They would," Hannah said quite simply. "If the traders at the fort knew you intended to do that, they'd kill you. They'll let nothing stand in their way. You must be very careful when dealing with the men at the fort. That's what North says."

Lily rose from the table. She'd already learned that lesson—the hard way.

After watching North clean up their supper dishes last night, she took over the task as best she could. Hannah stayed busy, but Lily was certain she watched her with a disapproving eye.

Afterward, Hannah left the cabin without a word. Lily saw that she'd put a plate of food in the oven warmer for her; she wouldn't return today.

Lily strolled to the corral and stood on the fence to pat the horses. They tolerated her touch for a moment before moving away. She milled around inside the barn, looking at the feed and equipment. In the stall near the door, she saw the two buffalo robes, cushioned by a pile of hay, North had slept under last night. She didn't want to imagine him lying there sleeping, so she left.

Outside again, Lily walked a short distance down

the trail that led away from the cabin. Leaves rustled in the breeze. Birds fluttered their wings. Unseen varmints scurried through the underbrush. She shaded her eyes against the bright sunlight and gazed in the direction of Bent's Fort.

It was out there, somewhere. She could find it, probably. She'd watched the trail carefully when North had brought her here.

Lily looked back at the dozen horses in the corral. She knew how to ride. All of Madame DuBois's students had learned.

Her heart beat a little faster. She could make it to the fort.

But then what? Unless she happened to arrive there just as a friendly family was pulling out headed east, what would she do?

Jacob Tanner floated into her mind. He'd help her. Surely he would. He'd been kind to her. He didn't frighten her, unlike most of the other men there did.

North would know where she'd gone, of course. He'd come for her immediately.

But would he bring her back to the cabin?

Raw fear spread through Lily at the thought that perhaps North might decide she was, as he'd insinuated, too much trouble.

What if he left her at the fort, in the hands of Hiram Fredericks and the other men? After the things Hannah had said, Lily knew she was lucky to have gotten away from them when she did.

Lily turned back and headed toward the cabin. Her shoulders sagged with the sure knowledge that the only way she'd ever leave this place was if North took her.

If, of course, North kept his word.

The morning and afternoon dragged by with a slowness Lily had never before experienced. Hannah didn't return. Lily's only company was an occasional nicker from one of the horses in the corral, and the chirps of a few birds high in the trees.

Lily had never felt so alone in her life. Growing up, she'd always been at school with lots of teachers and other girls around. On the wagon train there had been families nearby, always someone to talk to. Even at the fort, the sound of voices and conversations had hummed through the day and most of the night.

Here at the cabin, there was only silence and loneliness.

By the time the sun dipped toward the horizon, Lily's isolation had begun to prey harder upon her mind. What if something should happen to her while North was away? A snakebite or a coyote attack? Who would know? Who could help?

The cabin turned uglier by the moment. It wasn't a home; it wasn't even a real house. There wasn't one thing pretty about it.

And what if some renegade Indians, or an outlaw,

or an army deserter happened by the cabin? She had no way to defend herself. She'd be at the mercy of any madman who came along.

By the time darkness fell, Lily had worked herself into a near frenzy. She paced inside the small cabin, berating herself for not at least attempting to escape this morning when she had the chance. She wrung her fingers together, fearing that some sort of catastrophe might befall her, or that some man with less than honorable intentions might happen by.

Hoofbeats pounding the soft earth sounded from outside. Lily ran to the door and threw it open wide. North appeared astride a brown stallion, riding up to the barn.

Relief weakened Lily's knees. Thank God he was home. Yet how dare he leave her alone like this all day long? She hurried toward the barn.

"Where have you been?" she asked, the words coming out in a hot rush.

North swung down from the saddle. He looked dusty and tired.

Lily pressed her lips together. "I—I was alone here for the whole day, all by myself, and I was frightened and worried and—"

"Where's Hannah?" he asked, his gaze darting to the cabin.

"She was here earlier, but—"

North nodded, as if Hannah's appearance here this morning meant everything had been handled to his satisfaction. He looped the reins around a corral fence post.

Lily fought back the urge to shout at him.

"I tried to talk to your sister today," she said and stepped closer when he turned back to the saddle once more. "I truly did. But she doesn't want to learn etiquette or manners, or anything to do with the East, for that matter. She refuses."

North pulled off the saddle and blanket, and heaved it onto the top board of the corral fence. He opened the gate, led the stallion inside and slipped off the bridle. The horse rubbed his head against North's shirt.

"There's no point in my being here." Lily stepped in front of him as he left the corral and closed the gate. "Listen to me, will you? It's silly and stupid, and I want to leave."

"No," North said, as he walked past her toward the cabin.

Stunned, Lily just stood there watching, then hurried after him.

"Please, listen." She touched his arm and he stopped. In the light from the cabin windows she saw that he looked even more tired than she'd first imagined.

"I can't live here like this, frightened and scared and worried all the time," Lily said, emotion rising to nearly choke off her words. She struggled to keep going. "I hate this place—I hate it. I want to go to my aunt's in Virginia. Now."

Weariness showed in his face, yet he spoke gently. "We've already talked about this. When you've taught my sister, you can leave."

"Please." Lily caught his sleeve once more, desperation clawing at her. "Please let me go home. I'll...I'll...I'll do anything."

A moment passed before the meaning of her words dawned on North. Lily flushed and lowered her gaze. Humiliation burned her cheeks.

What had she become that she'd make such an offer? Only a few weeks ago, she'd never had even considered saying something like this.

But these were desperate times. Lily dared to raise her gaze to him once more.

"I told you what I want you for," North said, his voice low and soft. "Nothing else."

Tears swelled in Lily's eyes. She'd offered her most sacred possession—and he'd turned it down with hardly a thought.

"I hate you!" Lily burst into tears and ran back toward the barn.

North jumped in front of her, blocking her path. "Go into the cabin."

"No!" she sobbed. He thought she intended to run away, yet even with the desperate need to escape pulsing through her, she wouldn't attempt an escape in the dark. "I won't go into the cabin—not if you're going in there!"

"I'm hungry."

"I don't care!"

North drew in a slow breath. "I won't leave you outside crying," he softly said.

"No!" Lily dragged her palms down her wet cheek. She knew she was being childish, but couldn't stop her tears.

He sighed with resignation, then ducked into the cabin and brought out one of the wooden chairs. He placed it in the shadows beside the door.

"Sit. Cry as much as you please while I eat," he told her calmly.

Lily plopped down in the chair and turned her back to him as he disappeared into the cabin. Her tears continued, coming harder and harder, until she nearly lost her breath. She hiccupped as the waves of ragged emotion finally subsided.

Turning in the chair, she looked through the doorway at North standing in front of the stove, making himself something to eat. She hated this place. Hated it with a passion. She wanted to go home.

She'd tried everything. She'd attempted to run away, to reason with North. She'd even offered herself. He'd rejected her at every turn. He wouldn't let her leave until it suited him.

Unless—

The swirl of anger, frustration and hurt in Lily's

belly hardened to a knot of determination. Her tears stopped. She sniffed and sat up straighter in the chair, still watching North.

He was certain of what he wanted from her. Fine. She'd give it to him.

And he would rue the day he asked for an Eastern woman in his life.

She'd see to it.

Chapter Nine

Lily greeted the dawn with a determination she hadn't felt since leaving Saint Louis. She flung open the cabin door and strode across the yard to the barn, filled with new purpose.

She liked the feeling.

She'd lain awake most of the night refining the idea that had come to her while sitting outside the cabin last night crying. When she awakened at dawn, it had still seemed like a good idea. In fact, it was the best idea she'd had in weeks.

North would not feel the same, however, and the notion brought a little smile to her lips.

Both he and his sister had proven themselves to be stubborn, hardheaded people. If she was ever going to gain their cooperation, she needed a plan to deal with each of them.

For North, her idea was a simple one: she'd be so much trouble and such a disruption in his life, that he'd give up on his idea of her teaching Hannah and let her leave immediately.

But North seemed to have as much patience as stubbornness, so Lily had come up with an plan to deal with Hannah, as well.

She couldn't force the girl to learn manners, etiquette and Eastern ways. As she'd already told North numerous times, it was impossible to teach an unwilling student.

But, perhaps, she could make Hannah *want* to learn. To accomplish that, Lily decided, she'd start off by becoming her friend.

The thought had warmed Lily. She could surely use a friend.

When she reached the barn door it was closed, and she wasn't sure if North was up and going about his chores yet, so she knocked. When she heard nothing, she opened the door. It creaked and moaned in the early morning silence. She leaned her head inside.

"Hello? North? Hello?" When she got no answer, she tried once more. "North!"

"What!"

Lily stepped inside the barn and followed the grouchy response to the first stall. She stopped in her tracks as she saw North lying on a mound of hay, sandwiched between two buffalo robes, the top one barely reaching his hips.

His black hair hung loose around his shoulders and fanned across his bare chest.

And a fine chest it was. Smooth, muscular, wide. Just as the women on the wagon train had said. The sight made Lily's heart beat strangely faster.

Then her gaze darted to his shirt, trousers and long johns draped over the boards of the stall. She gasped.

Good gracious, he was naked.

And beautiful. If a man could be called beautiful, he was it.

"What? What's wrong?" North pushed himself up on his elbow and grabbed for the buffalo robe, ready to throw it aside and spring to his feet.

"Nothing's wrong!" She pushed out both palms, her cheeks heating. "Don't get up!"

He squinted at her, coming fully awake now, yet seemingly unconcerned that she'd caught him without a stitch of clothing on.

North dug his fists into his eyes, trying to wipe away the sleep, then looked up at her.

"What do you want?" he asked.

Lily touched her fingers to her forehead, trying desperately to remember why she'd come here. But all she could think of was his chest. That beautiful chest…

She gave herself a mental shake.

"Oh, yes." Lily cleared her throat, remembering the plan she'd hatched last night, then forced her face into what she hoped was a no-nonsense expression.

"We've lots to do today," she told him. "We must get an early start."

"Yeah, okay," he said, stifling a yawn. "As soon as I take care of the horses and—"

"Cancel your plans," Lily said briskly. "I'm going to start Hannah's training today, and for that I need your assistance."

"What for?"

"The cabin must be converted, of course," she said, flicking her wrist as if the answer were obvious.

"Conver—"

"Come along," Lily said. "I'm going to make breakfast for us."

North lurched forward. The buffalo robe slid farther down his leg. "*You're* going to cook? But you don't know how—"

"Better hurry," Lily called, and heard what she suspected were Cheyenne curse words as she scurried out the door.

North pushed off the buffalo robe and got to his feet. The chill of the morning air against his skin reminded him that he'd slept little last night; climbing beneath the warmth of the robes for another hour or so would have felt good.

Yesterday had been long, the trip arduous but necessary. Then he'd come home to Lily in tears.

His father never mentioned that Eastern women cried so often. He'd wanted to take her in his arms last night, hold her, comfort her. Tired though he was, a strange energy had filled him. He'd never experienced it before. Until now. Until Lily.

He didn't understand it.

North washed at the water bucket he'd brought inside the barn with him last night, and pulled on his long johns.

Yesterday's ride had given him hours—too many hours, really—to think, and what he'd thought most about was Lily. He wasn't all that proud that he'd forced her to come to his cabin, forced her to stay here and teach Hannah.

But he hadn't thought Lily would be so unhappy. Nor had he thought Hannah would be so reluctant.

Women…

North dragged on his trousers and slid his arms into the sleeves of his shirt. His plan was a good one. Why couldn't Lily and Hannah see that? Why did they fight him every step of the way?

For a while yesterday, North had considered forgetting the whole thing. He'd mulled it over, given it serious thought. It certainly would have made his life a lot easier, no question about it.

But the easy way was seldom the best way.

Long before his trip ended yesterday, he knew he couldn't let the tears and reluctance of two women stop him. What he intended to do was too important.

Whites and Indians had to learn to live together peacefully. How could that be accomplished except through education?

He couldn't abandon his plan.

Especially if the rumors he'd heard were true.

Pulling on his socks and boots, North tied his hair at his nape, his spirits lifting. From all appearances this morning, it seemed his worrying yesterday had been for nothing. Lily, apparently, had come around to his way of thinking. He didn't understand why, but he didn't want to ask, either.

All he knew was that Lily wasn't crying and that she was going to teach Hannah.

That was good enough.

He pulled his suspenders over his shoulders and headed for the cabin.

When North stepped inside, Lily looked up from the sheet of paper on the table in front of her. She tapped it with her pencil.

"We've got a lot to do today," she declared. "I've made a list."

"I thought you were making breakfast," North asked and gestured toward the cold stove.

"Eastern women don't really cook," Lily explained, wrinkling her nose at him and not bothering to mention that she'd eaten the food Hannah had made for her yesterday before going out to the barn and waking him.

"But I made coffee," she told him. "And there's some bread left from supper."

"I'm hungry. I—"

"Do you want to begin Hannah's training, or not?" Lily asked, standing up.

"Yes, but—"

"Then have some coffee and let's get started," Lily said, putting enthusiasm into her voice.

"Where's Hannah?" North's gaze swept the cabin. "Shouldn't she be here?"

"No, not really," Lily told him, dismissing his comment with a wave of her fingers. "I'm not quite ready for her yet. Not until everything here at the cabin is finished, that is."

North frowned. "Finished?"

"Yes. It must be turned into a proper Eastern household." Lily consulted the list she'd made on the sheet of paper before her. "First of all, everything must be moved outside for a thorough cleaning. You can start with the table."

He paused, his gaze zinging around the cabin. "Everything has to be moved outside? And you want me to move it?"

"Eastern women don't move furniture."

"But—"

"You do want me to teach Hannah. Right?"

"Yes, but—"

"And you do want her to learn to be a proper Eastern woman."

"Of course, but—"

"Then you'd better get moving." Lily put on a bright smile and tapped her finger against the table-top. "Starting right here."

While North sipped the coffee she'd made—which Lily was certain tasted absolutely dreadful—and moved the furniture out of the cabin, she went through some of the items in her trunk that the thieves at Bent's Fort hadn't taken. She was disheartened to see that so many of her nice things were gone.

"Could you move this trunk outside?" Lily called to North.

Sweat glistened on his forehead. He'd been moving household items out into the yard for a while now. He gave her a hard look, and for an instant she wondered if he'd balk at her latest request, but he lumbered across the cabin and picked up the trunk.

"You're doing an excellent job," she said cheerfully, and hurried out of the cabin ahead of him. "Just set it here, if you please."

North dropped the trunk on the table he'd already moved outside. She was sure he wanted to ask her what she wanted it for, but he didn't. He simply went back inside and continued to work.

When he'd finally moved all the furniture out, Lily had him empty every shelf and strip the bunk.

"Now, everything must be cleaned," she announced, waving her hands to encompass all the things that had been relocated outside, plus the interior of the cabin.

He gave her a sour look. "Let me guess. Eastern women don't clean."

"Of course not." She gave him a sweet smile. "Don't forget to rinse thoroughly."

North grumbled under his breath, and went back into the cabin.

Lily lifted the lid of the trunk and dug through it, noting which of her gowns were inside. She pawed to the bottom, relieved to find that her sewing kit had been overlooked by the thieves.

From the corner of her eye, she saw Hannah step out of the woods. The girl couldn't have come along at a better time. Lily struggled to hide her smile. Her plan was proceeding perfectly.

"Good morning," Lily called.

Hannah approached with a mixture of suspicion and caution on her face. "What are you doing?"

"Just looking at my dresses." Lily shut the trunk lid quickly, allowing Hannah only a glimpse of the colorful fabrics. She gestured inside the cabin. "North moved all the furniture outside for me this morning. Now he's cleaning."

"Cleaning? North is cleaning?" Hannah leaned sideways and gazed through the door. Her eyes widened. "But that's squaw work."

"Eastern women never do any heavy lifting," Lily explained. "Or cleaning."

"They don't?" Hannah looked slightly intrigued. "Why not?"

"It simply isn't done."

"But how do their houses get cleaned?" Hannah wanted to know.

"Servants. All high-society Eastern women have servants—many servants, in fact."

Hannah gazed inside at North again, then at all the furniture cluttering the yard, trying, it seemed, to take it all in, to understand. She opened her mouth, but Lily cut her off.

"You should just run along," Lily said kindly. "There's really nothing for you to do here today."

"Oh." Hannah hesitated, then headed off into the woods again.

Lily got out her paper and pencil, then pulled one of her dresses and the sewing kit from the trunk. She assembled everything on the table and went to work measuring, then sketched out a pattern. She wasn't sure how much time had passed before North came outside.

His sleeves were rolled back, his shirtfront and the knees of his trousers were soaked.

"Finished already?" Lily asked. She gave him a big smile. "My, you do quick work."

He threw her a look, then collapsed onto the ground beneath a large tree.

Lily sorted through the dishes piled on the seat of one of the chairs, found a tin cup and filled it from the water bucket beside the door. She took it to North.

He looked up at her. "What's this? Eastern women fetch water?"

"Just trying to do my part," she announced, and sat down on the soft grass beside him.

North took the cup and settled back against the tree trunk.

Gazing at him, Lily felt a pang of guilt. He'd come home tired last night, and she'd awakened him early this morning, then put him to work moving furniture and cleaning. Yet he'd muttered hardly a word of complaint.

His commitment to his plan that would send Hannah to the East was great. An admirable quality, Lily thought. Especially since he was willing to put up with her to accomplish it.

Yet she had a plan, too, and she wasn't ready to abandon it simply because of a few guilty qualms.

"Where were you all day yesterday?" Lily asked. "I was frightened here alone for so long."

"Frightened? Of what?"

"Wild animals," she told him, and gestured toward the woods. "Bears, coyotes—"

"Did you see a bear?"

"Well, no."

"A coyote?"

"No. But what if I had gotten hurt?" she proposed. "No one was here to help me."

"Did you get hurt?" he asked.

"I could have," she told him. "Or what if some stranger had come along? Someone whose intentions weren't honorable."

He narrowed his eyes. "Did you see a stranger?"

"That's not the point," she insisted.

North mulled it over for a moment. "So you were frightened of wild animals and strangers, and of getting hurt. Yet you didn't actually see any animals or strangers, nor were you hurt. You just constructed the fantasy in your mind, as in a dream."

When he said it like that, the whole thing sounded silly.

"I know that man who came to the cabin the other night wasn't a dream," Lily told him. "Who was he?"

"I have to tend to the horses." North pushed himself to his feet. "I'll make sure Hannah stays with you all day the next time I leave so you won't be afraid."

He walked away leaving Lily alone beneath the tree. He'd reached the barn before Lily realized that he hadn't told her where he'd gone yesterday. Nor had he explained about the mysterious midnight caller.

Chapter Ten

Lily hadn't seen North since early afternoon when she'd had him move all the furniture back into the cabin while she'd picked wildflowers at the edge of the forest. He'd left in a huff and she hadn't seen him since.

That was fine with her. She'd been too busy to deal with him, anyway.

Now, hours later with the lanterns blazing in the cabin, she assessed the improvements she'd made to the place.

Not bad, she decided, turning in a circle. Especially in view of the fact that she'd had only the fabric of her own dresses to work with, and a few of her personal items.

A yellow-and-pink cloth draped the table, with matching bows tied to the chairs. The wildflowers she'd picked this afternoon sat on the table in a white vase that had belonged to her mother. The pink-patterned china she'd brought with her from Saint Louis lined the shelves. Her books sat on the mantel, along with more flowers.

The last improvement she wanted to complete tonight was to hang the sunny yellow window curtains she'd fashioned from one of her day dresses. Lily slid a chair beneath the window and juggled the fabric, hammer and nails as she climbed up.

She'd had little experience using tools—Madame DuBois hadn't covered the subject—so she struggled to position the fabric correctly, and to hammer it into place. It wasn't long before her arms started to ache. She banged her own thumb. But finally, as she drove the final nail in place, the cabin door opened.

North walked inside. He stopped short and took in the room. His expression changed from startled, to confused, then finally, to anger.

"What have you done?" he demanded, his gaze impaling her.

The murderous look on his face froze Lily in place. She dropped the hammer.

"What have you done!" he repeated, this time at a near roar.

She whirled on the chair, lost her footing and tumbled backward. A scream died on her lips as she felt North's arms capture her, saving her from the fall.

He gathered her against him, snug against his

chest. Instinctively, Lily looped her arm around his neck and held on tight.

With her face mere inches from his, she gazed into his eyes—those dark, smoldering eyes of his—and suddenly, he didn't look angry at all. He looked as if—

Lily couldn't read his expression, yet somehow it called to her. She leaned closer, unable not to. Her body tingled where it touched his. His arms drew her nearer, tight against him.

He leaned closer until his lips hovered in front of hers. She could almost taste him already. Lily's heart thudded wildly in her chest, sure that he was going to kiss her.

Then, abruptly, North set her down and stalked out of the cabin.

Lily clutched her hand to her chest, as if she might slow the pounding of her heart, and stared at the empty doorway.

Had she been wrong in thinking North intended to kiss her?

Had she been wrong in *wanting* him to?

Holding on to the back of the chair to steady herself, Lily willed herself to calm down and tried to figure out what, exactly, had just happened. But all she knew for sure was that North had been angry when he'd seen what she'd done to his cabin.

Which was what she'd been after all along.

Drawing in a breath, Lily walked outside. She

stood near the door for a moment while her eyes adjusted to the darkness, expecting to see North at the barn. Instead, she found him standing in the shadow of the cabin, looking up at the stars.

"I take it you don't like my improvements to the cabin," she ventured, stopping close to him.

North turned to her but didn't answer. She wondered once again if he didn't understand what she'd said, or if he was purposely trying to vex her.

Despite the plan she'd come up with, Lily felt the urge to defend what she'd done.

"You want Hannah to learn Eastern ways," Lily told him. "I simply provided the proper environment in which she can do that."

"You should have discussed it with me first," he said.

Yes, she probably should have—and would have, had her purpose not been to annoy him.

North moved closer, a predatory look in his eye. Yet it didn't startle her. Instead, it called to her to stand her ground—and think that the incident with the cabin had left his mind completely.

Gently, he touched his palm to her cheek, stroking her jaw with his fingers as he gazed into her eyes. Lily's heart rose in her throat. He slid his hand around to her nape and dug his fingers softly into her hair. He pulled her closer, then leaned down and kissed her.

His mouth covered hers with a warmth and tenderness that sent her heart racing. He blended their lips together, tasting her, sampling her. Lily sighed and leaned her head back. She latched onto his shoulder to keep from falling. North looped his arm around her waist and pulled her tight against him.

Her breasts brushed his hard chest, weakening her knees. Her thighs touched his. North groaned and deepened their kiss.

Then, as quickly, he lifted his head. His ragged breath puffed hot against her mouth. For a moment, she thought he intended to kiss her again, but instead he released her and backed away.

North had left her standing in the shadows last night, her lips wet with his kiss, her body trembling—and he'd simply walked away. Was that the proper etiquette for the situation? Lily couldn't recall Madame DuBois covering that topic in any of her classes.

She pushed the final pin into her hair and glanced out the window. She hadn't seen North yet this morning. Was he still sleeping?

The vision of his bare chest and long hair flashed in her mind, bringing a little tingle with the recollection. Lily forced the images from her mind. Good gracious, what was she thinking so early in the morning?

By the time she'd finished dressing, Hannah came

into the cabin. She stopped in the doorway, froze much as North had last night, and took in the room.

"What do you think?" Lily asked. When Hannah didn't respond immediately, she went on, "I wanted the cabin to have a look and feel similar to my home back East. Do you like it?"

"It's…nice," Hannah said, though Lily thought she was just being polite.

Hannah lifted the corner of the tablecloth and rubbed the fabric slowly between her fingers. "It's very soft," she said.

"I cut up several of my dresses," Lily explained, gesturing to her trunks beside the bunk.

"Could—could I see them?" Hannah asked.

"Certainly. Sometime," Lily said, dismissing the subject. "Right now, I'd like to ask you for some help. I'd really like to learn to cook. Would you be willing to teach me?"

Hannah raised her eyebrows, surprised. "You want *me* to teach *you?*"

"If I learn to take care of myself, you won't have to come here anymore," Lily pointed out.

Hannah hesitated, then apparently seeing the value in Lily's suggestion, told her, "I can do that. I can teach you."

"Good. Let's get started."

Hannah began breakfast preparation with Lily at her elbow, watching and listening to her instructions. While the food cooked, Lily kept herself busy

setting the table with her china service and the napkins she'd made that matched the tablecloth.

"This china service belonged to my mother,"
Lily explained, setting the plates on the table. "She
had it specially designed for her in England many
years ago, right after she married my father. They
went there on their honeymoon."

Hannah studied the china for a moment, but didn't
say anything.

When the eggs, ham and potatoes finished cooking, Lily placed them on a serving platter in the
center of the table. Just as they were about to sit,
North came inside.

Hannah's mouth turned down at the sight of him,
contempt clouding her features.

He stopped just inside the door and looked over
the room, then winced and shook his head.

"I think it's pretty," Hannah blurted out.

North looked surprised, then pulled out the chair
and sat down at the table. He eyed the pink-
patterned plate before him, picked it up, felt its
weight, and frowned his disapproval.

"Lily's mother had these dishes made for her,"
Hannah told him, none too politely, as she sat down.
"They came all the way from England."

Lily took the chair across from Hannah. "This is
an Eastern household now, so we will all use our
napkins at every meal."

But instead of directing her comments to Hannah,

Lily picked up North's napkin, snapped it open and presented it to him. His expression darkened, as if daring her to drape it across his lap. Lily flushed at the thought. She dropped it on the table beside his plate and turned her attention back to her meal.

When they'd finished eating, North left the cabin. Lily was relieved. The man always seemed to unnerve her in the strangest ways.

She spent the day with Hannah. The young girl was quite competent at everything it took to run a house, feed and clothe herself and a family.

"Where did you learn all these things?" Lily asked, as they gathered berries in the woods near the cabin.

"From my mother," Hannah said, "and the women of our tribe."

"I'm sure you've made your mother very proud," she said, then paused, fearing that her comment was inappropriate. "Your mother, is she still alive?"

Hannah pulled several more berries from the bush and dropped them into her basket. "Yes. My father likes to explore. He's gone West and my mother is with him. She always goes with him."

"Oh, my…" Lily said, trying to imagine a woman strong enough to routinely make such a journey. "She must love your father very much to live that sort of life."

"She has no English china to carry with her." Hannah grinned and popped a berry into her mouth.

Lily smiled with her, then looked down at her basket. ''Well, do you think we have enough to—''

Hannah touched her fingers to Lily's lips, silencing her, then grabbed her hand and pulled her behind a large tree. Alarm spread through Lily as she mimicked Hannah, standing still and quiet.

A voice, faint in the distance, caught Lily's attention. She leaned around the tree, searching for its origin. Hannah pulled her back and frowned a warning, but not before Lily had caught a glimpse of two men walking through the woods together. North, and someone she didn't know.

Surely, Hannah recognized North's voice, it was distinctive as the men drew nearer. Yet she stayed behind the tree, out of sight.

The voices grew louder. Hannah crouched. She pulled Lily down with her.

A few yards away, North walked past their hiding place. The man with him was tall, broad shouldered, dressed in dark trousers and a white shirt. Lily saw only the side of his face as the men walked farther into the woods; she still didn't recognize him.

After their voices faded, Hannah held her position for a few moments longer, then rose and caught Lily's arm, pulling her up, too.

''We must go,'' Hannah whispered urgently.

She was quick and surefooted through the trees and underbrush. Lily hurried to keep up.

"Who was that man with North?" Lily asked, after they'd gone a ways.

"You musn't speak of it." Hannah's words were harsh. "Ever."

Lily wanted to ask more, but sensed she'd get nothing further from Hannah. She'd ask North himself.

That evening after supper, while North was in the barn tending to the horses, Lily asked Hannah if she'd stay at the cabin for the night and continue with her cooking instructions the next day. Hannah agreed more easily than Lily had hoped.

"If Eastern women don't cook or clean," Hannah asked, as she dried the last of the supper dishes, "what do they do all day?"

"Lots of things," Lily said, shaking the dishwater from her hands and picking up a linen towel. "Organize charity events, help the needy and the less fortunate, work on committees to improve our city."

Hannah gave her a sideways look. "You must spend a lot of your time getting dressed."

Lily looked down at herself and grinned. "That's true," she said, and felt a pang of envy at Hannah's simple clothing.

Exhausted after the long day, Hannah made a bed for herself on buffalo robes spread out in front of the fireplace. She fell asleep immediately. Lily slipped outside, looking for North. She found him stretched out on the ground, hands clasped behind his neck, gazing up at the stars.

At her approach, he sat up quickly, turned his head to catch the sound, though she was certain he could have heard nothing more than the brush of her shoes across the soft grass.

"It's only me," she said.

He looked up at her. "I wasn't sure, since you weren't talking."

Lily uttered a laugh at his gentle barb. She waited for a moment for him to ask her to sit down beside him, but when he didn't, she sat down anyway.

"Does my talking bother you?" she asked, smoothing down her skirt.

"Now you're going to talk about talking?" North shook his head, but didn't sound so offended that it deterred her from carrying on with a conversation.

"Who was that man you were walking through the woods with today?" she asked.

North turned to her. "What were you doing in the woods?"

"Picking berries," she said, "and don't change the subject. Who was he?"

He gazed out across the darkened expanse toward the woods. "I trade horses. I talk to lots of men."

North hadn't met her eye when he'd spoken, which was unlike him, and that caused Lily to wonder if he was being honest.

"Hannah didn't seem to like him," she said, hoping to prod more information from him.

"I don't like him, either," North said, and from the tone of his voice she knew he spoke the truth now. "I wouldn't give him one of my horses."

"Why not?"

"I'm particular about what I trade for." North looked down at her and grinned. "You, of all people, should know that."

Lily flushed, pleased by the compliment. "I never thanked you for settling my debts at the fort."

North just looked at her.

"So, thank you."

"You're welcome," he whispered.

Their gazes met and held for a long moment. North leaned closer, and Lily thought he intended to kiss her again.

Should she let him? It wasn't the proper thing to do, but—

He kissed her.

And she let him.

Lily moaned softly as his lips took hers in a most delightful exchange. He dipped his head to trail kisses down her jaw, to the curve in her neck, muzzling her soft flesh. When he broke away, the naked yearning on his face startled her...pleased her.

"Lily, I—" North stopped. He drew back from her and let out a long slow breath, then got to his feet. "I'm going to the fort tomorrow."

Disappointment filled her unexpectedly. "You'll be gone all day?"

"Most of the day."

Lily got to her feet. "Can I go with—"

"No. I have business there. I'll make sure Hannah stays with you."

Lily didn't bother to ask again or argue. She knew it would do no good.

"Will you take a letter for me?" Lily asked. "I want to tell my aunt in Richmond about my father. I'm sure she's wondering about what's going on out here."

North nodded, then shifted his weight from one foot to the other. His gaze bounced around. When it landed on Lily again, it seemed to burn with passion. He caught her shoulders, kissed her quickly on the mouth, then turned and disappeared into the night.

Chapter Eleven

Now what?

North hesitated outside the cabin as Lily beckoned him. Just behind her stood Hannah. From the wide smiles on their faces, he knew they were up to something.

Again.

For over a week now, Lily and Hannah had been nearly inseparable. They took walks in the woods and came home with berries, apples, plums. They spent hours in the cabin, cooking, cleaning, doing something—North didn't know what, exactly.

And they talked. Lord, how the two women talked.

He'd never heard Hannah chatter so much until Lily came along.

They giggled together, too. He often heard them laughing inside the cabin. But when he'd walked inside to join in, they both quieted. Hannah was still mad at him for wanting to send her back East.

"Come in. Come inside. We have a surprise for you," Hannah insisted, waving him toward the cabin. "You'll like it."

"I hope," Lily murmured.

What had they done to his cabin now? He couldn't imagine. North was almost afraid to walk inside and find out.

When he'd first seen the changes Lily had made to his home, he'd been furious. Bows and ruffles everywhere. Curtains on the windows. Flowers sitting in bottles for no apparent reason.

Now, though, he'd gotten used to things being different, and, truthfully, it no longer bothered him. In fact, the cabin was rather nice to walk into now. It looked pretty. And so did Lily. It smelled nice…like Lily.

She came forward and grasped his arm, drawing him inside the cabin; her touch sent a rush all the way up to his shoulder.

Hannah gestured grandly at the table.

"Lily made supper," she announced. "Her first meal—all by herself!"

Lily blushed, and gave him a hopeful smile.

North looked over the pots and pans simmering on the stove, steam rising from them, the pink dishes already placed on the table atop a colored cloth.

There were flowers in a jar sitting right in the middle of the table.

He wasn't sure why Lily made such a fuss about eating. The Eastern tradition that suggested every meal should be a special occasion seemed odd to him. Everyone gathered around the table at a specific time, eating just-prepared food, following a rigid regimen of customs—"manners," Lily had called them. North didn't see the need for such a big production for simply satisfying hunger.

The women of his tribe made food available throughout the day. Pots of soup or stew cooked over a fire ready for anyone to consume when they chose. They ate directly from the common pot, sometimes dipping bread the women cooked on hot flat stones.

Still, the look of accomplishment on Lily's face pleased him.

"You cooked all of this yourself?" he asked her, not bothering to hide his surprise. "That's good."

"You haven't tasted it yet," Lily pointed out with a wry smile.

"Sit down," Hannah instructed, pulling him toward the table.

North settled into the chair and breathed in the rich aroma of the food.

When he'd first learned that Lily wanted to cook, he'd been stunned. He thought she'd quit after a day or so, but she hadn't, and for some reason that had compelled him to step up his hunting.

Now he tracked only the best game, the fattest geese and duck. She'd asked him to bring home a turkey but North had refused. Indians didn't eat turkey, believing the meat would turn warriors into cowards and cause them to run from their enemies.

He'd made another trip to the fort and traded for extra rations of pork, beef, cheese, rice, beans, vegetables and indulged in the luxury of sugar and molasses. He'd considered bringing down a buffalo for her.

Lily served the food with a look of deep concentration on her face. He'd seen that same expression this past week when he'd come into the cabin, pretending to look for something, or clean his rifle, just to watch her at the stove.

Graceful movements, even as she pushed a stray lock of hair behind her ear, stirred a pot, stretched up to retrieve something from a high shelf. And her hands—soft, small, delicate. No calluses.

What would her hands feel like against his skin? Sometimes North laid awake at night wondering.

Sometimes he laid awake at night wishing he didn't have to wonder.

"Taste it," Hannah urged.

With both women watching, North sliced off a bite of the duck she'd roasted. He chewed slowly, thoughtfully, then nodded.

"It's good." He looked at Lily and tried—unsuccessfully—to hide his genuine surprise. "It's really good."

She smiled and nodded at Hannah. "I had an excellent teacher."

The meal did taste good, Lily decided as they ate. But perhaps her sense of accomplishment enhanced the flavor. North's praise hadn't hurt anything, either.

When they finished, Hannah helped clear the table. North lingered.

"Can I give you a hand?" he asked, waving toward the dirty dishes.

"We can handle everything," Lily said.

"The ladies are running the house," Hannah informed him with a twist of her chin.

"Besides," Lily said, trying to soften his sister's words, "I'm certain you have things to take care of at the barn."

"I've been working on repairing the wagon, but it can wait. I can—"

"We don't need you," Hannah said.

He stood there for another moment as if he felt left out, then finally went outside.

"Would you like to make a pie tomorrow?" Hannah asked, lifting the wash bucket. "North bought extra sugar at the fort."

"Let's do," Lily agreed. She paused, studying Hannah in the lantern light. "Can you believe I spent the largest part of my life in school, and I never learned to do what you taught me this past week?''

"It was a different sort of school, wasn't it?'' Hannah asked.

"Yes, but what a waste. All those years of learning little more than social acceptance. Nothing that helped me—or anyone else.'' Lily shook her head. "But you…my, how I envy you.''

Hannah paused, elbow deep in the dishwater. "Why?''

"Because you have the opportunity to do something truly meaningful for the people of your tribe.''

Her brows drew together. "You mean if I do as North wants and go back East?''

"Yes,'' Lily said, taking the last of the dishes from the table.

Hannah turned back to the washtub and scrubbed all the plates before she looked up again.

"Do you think I could do it?'' she asked. "Learn everything, I mean, and go back East and talk about our ways and customs.''

Lily nodded solemnly. "Hannah, you can do *anything*.''

"Looks like we've got company.''

At North's words, Lily turned and followed his gaze to the edge of the forest. She'd come outside to talk to him about Hannah, interrupting his repairs to the covered wagon, but the two figures who materialized among the trees took her attention.

Men come to trade, she guessed. Or perhaps messengers from the fort. She doubted they were people simply passing through. Nobody passed through, out here in the middle of nowhere.

Lily glanced up at North. No trepidation or concern showed on his face, making her think they were welcome guests.

But when they stepped clear of the woods, Lily's heart lurched. A woman. One of them was a woman. Young, white, wearing a dress of rough calico. Slightly in front of her walked a grizzly bear of a man, dressed in buckskins, sporting a wooly beard and wild hair.

"Tom Carson," North said to Lily. "His wife, Grace. They live a few miles away."

"A few miles?" Lily wanted to hit him. A woman—no older than herself—had lived close by all these weeks, and North had never told her? Someone very much like her, whom she could have talked to, commiserated with? Another woman who could have relieved the desperate ache of isolation she'd at times endured?

The Carsons stopped halfway across the yard, waiting to be acknowledged. Lily wanted to rush to greet them, but reined in her patience and walked alongside North. The men shook hands, and introductions were made.

"I'm so happy to meet you," Lily said to Grace, and she'd never meant anything more in her life. Grace clasped her outstretched hands, seemingly as pleased to see another woman as Lily was.

"I didn't know you had yourself a wife now," Tom said to North.

Lily's gaze collided with North's. It was a logical assumption. They were, after all, living there at the cabin together. Yet it startled Lily and caused her cheeks to heat.

"I'm a visitor here," she said.

Tom's brow rose and his lips quirked.

"She's a teacher," North told him, "here for my sister."

Tom nodded, as if hearing the explanation, but not believing it.

Lily fought off the urge to explain further. "Would you care for some refreshment?"

"I've come to talk a little business," Tom said to North and nodded toward the horses in the corral. "If you've got the time, that is."

"Please, Grace, come inside," Lily invited, gesturing toward the cabin.

Grace hesitated. She turned to her husband, her gaze not meeting his. "Is it all right?"

Tom mulled it over. "I reckon," he finally said. "For a few minutes."

"I'm truly glad to see you," Lily said as she and

Grace hurried toward the cabin. "I had no idea you lived close by."

Grace smiled broadly. "I haven't seen another woman in months. I couldn't believe it when we walked up to the cabin and I saw you—"

Her words died as they stepped inside. Grace gasped and touched her fingers to her lips. She turned, taking in the room wide eyed.

"Oh…oh, it's lovely," Grace declared. "Did you do all of this?"

Lily smiled modestly. "Yes."

"And North didn't mind?"

"Well, let's just say he got used to the idea," Lily told her.

"Oh, my…"

Hannah appeared in the doorway, her arms loaded with firewood. She hesitated, eyeing Grace with a fair amount of suspicion.

"Come inside, Hannah." Lily waved her into the cabin and introduced her to Grace. "Let's all have some coffee."

Hannah dumped the logs in the wood box beside the stove and helped Lily serve.

"We made a pie this morning," Lily said, "but it isn't quite cool enough yet."

"You came all the way out here for a teaching position?" Grace asked.

Lily smiled. "Actually, Hannah is teaching me right now."

"And after your duties here are completed?" Grace asked. "What will you do, then?"

"Go back home, of course," Lily said. "That is, I'm going to live with my aunt in Richmond."

The three women took seats around the table with their coffee cups.

"Have you lived here long?" Lily asked, stirring in a little sugar.

"About a year now." Grace forced a smile. "It was Tom's idea to come here right after we were married. An adventure, he said. Just the two of us. My father is somewhat well-off. He outfitted us for the journey. Tom is a trapper and fur trader."

"Where are you from?" Lily asked.

"Maryland. Papa owns a factory there."

Lily shook her head. "This is a very long way from Maryland."

Grace gave her a quick smile and sipped her coffee. "So how do you like it here?"

"It's been an…adjustment," Lily admitted. "I came here with my father. We intended to start a business in Santa Fe, but he died at the fort. North offered me the…opportunity…to teach Hannah."

She knew it was only a partial truth, but Lily didn't see the need to tell Grace that she'd been bartered like so much livestock, and couldn't leave this place until her debt was settled with North.

"It's lonely here," Lily said. She smiled at Hannah beside her. "Luckily, I have company."

"Oh, yes, you're very fortunate," Grace agreed. She ran her palm along the tablecloth. "This fabric is beautiful. Did you find it at the fort?"

"Actually, it's one of my dresses."

Grace's eyes widened, a mixture of awe and envy. "It must have broken your heart to take scissors to such a beautiful gown."

"I needed a tablecloth more than a gown." Lily nodded toward her trunks in the corner. "I have other dresses. Would you like to see them?"

"Could I?"

"Certainly." Lily rose from the chair and Grace hurried after her.

Lily looked back to see Hannah still seated at the table. "Would you like to see them, too?"

She nodded quickly and hurried over.

Lily dropped to her knees and lifted the lid of her trunk. Grace pulled up a footstool and Hannah settled herself on the floor.

The other women gasped as Lily pulled the first gown from the trunk. It was a promenade dress of deep-green silk, the full skirt trimmed with broad bias bands of matching velvet. The plain sleeves, loose over the elbow, featured a broad velvet band. The undersleeves were of batiste.

"It's beautiful..." Grace declared.

The next gown Lily produced was gray satin, with seven flounces, trimmed with silk cord. Then from the trunk she lifted a promenade dress of lilac satin, featuring a skirt decorated with three deep tucks.

"This is my favorite," Lily said.

"Lovely," Grace agreed.

The final gown was a deep-blue silk, the skirt bordered with one large ruffle, trimmed with velvet bows.

Looking back, Lily wondered why she'd packed so many gowns. They were hardly appropriate—or useful—in the harsh wilderness. Yet at the time, she'd hadn't known any better. Another hard lesson of the Trail.

Grace sighed with pleasure at the beautiful gowns and accessories—lace gloves, a black velvet shawl and bonnet, a beaded handbag.

"You can try them on, if you'd like," Lily offered.

Grace stroked the soft velvet of the shawl. "Oh, no, I shouldn't."

"Really, it's fine," Lily insisted, and genuinely meant it. "You too, Hannah."

"They're beautiful," Hannah admitted, running a silk ruffle between her fingers.

Grace slipped the shawl around her shoulders and tied on the bonnet. She rose and turned in a slow, graceful circle. "How do I look?"

"Beautiful!" Lily declared.

The women all laughed together.

"Try on a dress," Lily said to Hannah.

"Oh, yes, do," Grace agreed. "Here. Take the blue one. It will look lovely with your light hair."

Hannah lifted the gown and held it up in front of her, the yards of fabric fanning out around her. "But I don't know where to begin...."

"I'll help," Lily told her.

She dug through her satchel and came up with undergarments. Hannah was slightly smaller than she, but they should fit well enough. "You'll need these."

"I'll fix your hair," Grace offered.

Hannah hesitated another moment, then said, "Well, all right."

Talking nonstop, giggling occasionally, Lily and Grace got Hannah into the gown, then styled her hair atop her head with combs and pins. When they were satisfied they'd done all the could, they stepped back and looked at their handiwork.

"You're lovely...." Lily whispered.

Grace nodded. "You look like a princess."

Hannah ran her palms down the silk skirt. She turned slowly, feeling the movement of the dress, hearing the rustle of the petticoats.

"It's beautiful." She gave Lily a tentative smile. "Do Eastern women dress like this often?"

"All the time," Lily said. "Even fancier, for parties and special occasions."

"For the Christmas ball one year, I had an ivory

gown trimmed with red velvet." Grace smiled at the memory. "Oh, I felt so beautiful that night."

The cabin door opened and North stepped inside. He stopped short, eyeing the women across the room.

Lily couldn't blame him. She had on elbow-length lace gloves, Grace wore a velvet shawl and bonnet, and Hannah was dressed for a ball.

North went ahead as if nothing were amiss. "I asked Tom to have supper with us. Could you—"

His brows drew together. He stepped farther inside the cabin. "Hannah?"

All three women giggled. Hannah blushed.

"Isn't she lovely?" Lily asked.

"I didn't even recognize..." North walked closer, looking his sister up and down. "You really are beautiful. Just as our father described his sisters back East. I wish he could see you. I wish *our aunts* could see you."

Hannah shrugged. "Maybe they can."

Chapter Twelve

Lily noted that Hannah said little through supper, Grace hadn't spoken at all and North was his customary reticent self. None of that surprised Lily, since Tom Carson seemed determined to do most of the talking.

She didn't especially like the man, and sensed that Hannah felt the same. Yet there must have been something redeeming about Tom Carson if North invited him to sit down at his table and share a meal.

A meal that was proving difficult to sit through.

A great portion of Lily's training at Madame DuBois's academy in Saint Louis centered on entertaining guests, and the responsibility of the hostess to steer supper-table discussions to palatable subjects and ensure that everyone was included in the conversation.

Even Madame DuBois herself would have been challenged at this table, Lily decided.

"That ol' buzzard Benton is bound and determined to ruin everything for us out here," Tom grumbled, as he pushed another spoonful of beans into his mouth.

"Thomas Hart Benton?" Lily asked. "The senator from Missouri?"

"Just like everybody back East," Tom complained, neither acknowledging nor answering Lily's question. "Wanting to come out here, take things over from us, run the place their own way."

"I overheard talk about Senator Benton at the fort," Lily said. "He's in favor of expanding U.S. land west of the Rockies. I take it, Mr. Carson, that you don't agree with him?"

"You're damned right I don't agree with it, and neither does any other businessman out here." Tom planted his elbow on the table and looked hard at Lily. "You didn't hear anybody at the fort saying they wanted more government interference out here, now did you?"

"Well, no," Lily told him.

"The very last thing we need," Tom complained, "is the government out here nosing in, taking over, passing laws, cutting into our businesses, our profits, telling us how to do things."

"But the government might bring order," Lily offered. "Make the territory safer for settlers and businessmen alike."

Tom didn't bother to respond, just waved away

her comment with his hand. His brows drew together. "At the fort the other day, I heard that the army is mounting a westward expedition. And you know what that means."

Without waiting for anyone to comment, Tom went on, "It means trouble. Serious trouble for those soldiers—and anybody trying to help them."

A chill swept up Lily's spine as the supper table fell silent.

"Do you mean—?"

"What I mean is," Tom said, "that anybody caught passing on information to the army that would help their expedition, better start looking for a new place to live, if they know what's good for them."

During their walks in the woods, Hannah had told her many of the same things Tom had just said, but hearing them from this man made the dire predictions seem even more ominous.

After supper, North and Tom went outside while the women cleared the table and washed the dishes.

"I'm sorry about Tom," Grace said quietly, glancing toward the door. "He's adamant about no government intervention out here."

"He's not the only one," Lily pointed out.

"He's been railing about the army expedition since he heard the rumor at the fort. He almost got into a fight about it with one of the settlers. And his threats about anyone at the fort helping with the expedition? It frightens me.'' Grace shook her head. ''I think the idea is a good one. A government presence out here would bring civilization—real towns, schools, churches. But I don't dare say that to Tom.''

Lily thought she was wise to keep her opinion to herself in front of her husband.

The women stayed in the cabin until Tom stuck his head inside and announced that it was time to leave. Lily walked outside with Grace, clinging to the last few minutes they could share. After only a few hours together, Lily felt as if she'd found a lifelong friend.

Just outside the cabin door, Grace turned suddenly and clamped her hand around Lily's forearm. ''Please, promise me something,'' Grace whispered.

Startled, Lily nodded. ''Of course. Anything.''

Grace glanced at Tom across the yard talking with North.

''Please, promise me you won't go back East without telling me,'' Grace begged. ''Please.''

''Of course—''

''I can't bear the thought of being alone out here again.'' Grace gulped, tears suddenly welling in her eyes. She glanced at her husband once more. ''Tom won't—''

''Let's go!'' Tom called.

Grace swiped her eyes quickly and turned to leave. Lily caught her arm.

"What is it, Grace? What's wrong?" she asked.

"Nothing," she whispered, then hurried away.

At the edge of the forest, Grace turned back quickly and waved, then disappeared into the woods after Tom. Worry and concern went with her, as Lily watched them leave. She wanted to run after Grace, ask her what she'd meant, but sensed it would do her new friend no good.

After a few moments, she realized North had come to stand beside her.

"Are you trading Mr. Carson one of your horses?" she asked.

"Two horses."

Surprised, she looked up at him. "I don't like that man."

"Why not?"

Lily shrugged. Other than the fact that he made terrible suppertime conversation and displayed poor table manners, she had no solid reason for her feelings. They were simply that: feelings.

"Do you like him?" Lily asked.

"Well enough to trade my horses."

"And invite to supper."

North looked troubled. "I thought you'd want his wife to stay."

Lily's stomach fluttered. "You invited him to supper just so I could visit longer with Grace? You did that? For…me?"

"I don't want you to be unhappy here," North told her. "I understand it's…difficult for you."

"Oh, North…that's the nicest thing anyone has ever done for me," Lily said, tears welling in her eyes.

"Don't cry." He waved his hands, looking a bit frantic. "Don't…please…"

A giggle sprang up, chasing away the threat of tears. "I can't help it," she said. "It was very sweet of you to do that for me."

"Keep it to yourself," North said with a frown. "I'm a hard-nosed horse trader. I don't want my reputation getting ruined."

"It was nice having people here for supper," Lily said. "It reminded me of back home, living in Saint Louis. On holidays when the school was closed, I'd stay with Papa and we'd have company. The house was beautifully decorated for the occasion. We'd use Mama's china service, and everyone would be dressed in their finest."

"You miss your home," North said.

Lily nodded. Sadness settled around her heart. "I thought Papa and I would have a home in Santa Fe. A place we could build together. I'd sketched some ideas for a house."

"A home isn't a roof over your head. It's a place in your heart," North said.

Lily changed the subject, not wanting, for some reason, to think that he might be right.

"Is it true what Tom Carson said about the army?" she asked. "Are they planning a Western expedition for the government?"

North shrugged. "That's the rumor going around the fort. Most of the men there aren't happy about it, as Carson said."

"But do they really dislike the notion enough to do harm to anyone helping the army?"

North nodded. "Anyone giving the government maps of the Western area, trails, passes, the location of rivers, would provide a valuable service to the expedition."

"And hurry Western expansion along considerably," Lily concluded. She shook her head. "Anyone doing that would be putting his own life in danger."

North didn't respond. After a moment, he said, "I'm glad to see you and Hannah are getting along well now."

"She's been wonderful company for me, but..." Lily's shoulders slumped. "I thought she was coming around, that she was finally willing to go along with your plan and let me start teaching her. But as soon as we finished the supper dishes, she took off again, back to the Cheyenne village, I suppose."

"She'll come around," North said. "Don't worry if it takes a while longer. Hannah will realize it's the right thing to do, and she'll go along with the idea."

"I hope you're right," Lily said, then went back toward the cabin.

North lingered in the yard, wanting to go inside with her, but holding back, watching.

He liked to watch her walk. She seemed to float, somehow. The wide skirts she wore billowed around her, hiding her hips, legs, ankles and feet. North wondered why Eastern women wore such odd-shaped clothing. Did they fear that, upon seeing a woman's true figure, men might become overwhelmed by desire for them? Lose all control?

The craving that had plagued him since the first moment he'd laid eyes on Lily made its presence known once more, with as much intensity as ever. North deliberately pulled his gaze from Lily's trim waist as she disappeared through the cabin door.

Maybe Eastern women were wise to keep their bodies covered, after all.

His thoughts floated to Grace Carson. He remembered seeing her last summer, shortly after she and her husband had arrived here from the East. They'd been at the fort, trading for goods. Young, obviously in love, green to the ways of the West.

He hardly recognized her today. She seemed to have aged considerably this past year. Her dark hair had lost its luster, her skin had reddened, then hardened, in the sun. And her hands. Rough, callused. So unlike Lily's soft delicate ones.

A jolt startled North. Was that what Lily would

look like in a year's time? The idea sickened him, yet he knew it was possible. The land here was hard, the life unforgiving. Only the hearty survived; only a few of the hearty flourished.

Would Lily be a survivor? The first moment he'd seen her at the fort, he knew what sort of woman she was. Weak. Delicate.

Trouble.

Yet she'd surprised him, more than once. She'd fought him—actually physically struggled against him—in an attempt to escape when he'd first brought her here. She'd taken on the challenge of Hannah. She'd learned to cook, to fend for herself. She could have wilted in this harsh place, but instead she'd pushed ahead.

Yet how long would that last? In a few month's time, would she look like Grace Carson, shriveled, hardened, beaten down by life?

She had to leave. North's chest tightened with the realization, yet he knew it was for the best. Lily didn't belong here. She belonged in the East, in a fine home, surrounded by beautiful things. This wasn't the life for her.

Though he wished with all his heart that it could be.

Chapter Thirteen

North raised the ax over his head and brought it down on the log, splitting it cleanly in two. Perspiration soaked his shirt and trickled down his temple. His shoulders ached and his back strained, but he didn't stop. He couldn't.

Chopping firewood, the most grueling physical labor, kept him from thinking, usually. It eased the tension that wound his gut into a tight knot, usually.

But neither of those things had been eased by the strenuous work. He'd been chopping wood for two straight days, and still he was thinking of—and wanting—Lily.

North dropped the head of the ax onto the ground and dragged his sleeve across his forehead. His gaze darted to the cabin, and determinedly, he pulled it back. Lily was inside.

He'd made a point to stay as far away from her as he could since the Carsons stopped by two days ago. They'd barely spoken. But, somehow, that only made him think of her more often.

He never should have kissed her. North picked up the ax and slammed it into another log. He never should have done it. What was the matter with him? What the hell had he been thinking?

And why did he want her? That was the greatest mystery of all. She was all wrong for him, for his way of life, for the land, for the West. She didn't belong here. She didn't want to be here.

He had to let her go. North drove the ax into the chopping block and left it there. He'd promised her she could go to her aunt's home in Virginia. He'd given his word. But still...

A sweet breeze tickled his nose, and he knew before he turned toward the cabin that it was Lily walking toward him. Nothing on the prairie smelled like Lily.

She had on a dark-blue dress; the color reminded him of the spring sky just before a rain shower. Her hair was piled atop her head, with little wisps of it curling around her face in the afternoon breeze.

She didn't belong here.

Once again, the truth slammed into North's belly along with his nearly overwhelming desire for her. He grabbed the ax and started chopping wood again.

How rude, Lily thought as she approached North and the wood shed. He saw her coming—she knew that he had—and he'd deliberately begun chopping wood again. He'd been chopping for two full days now—chopping like a madman.

The woodshed wouldn't hold much more, yet he kept at it. She didn't understand what the big attraction was here, but she needed to talk to him and he'd been elusive for the past two days. She wasn't waiting any longer.

Lily stopped in front of him and waited to be acknowledged. He ignored her. She folded her arms in front of her and glared at him.

He didn't look up. "I'm busy."

"We need—"

"Not now."

"Then when?" she demanded. "After you've chopped down the entire forest?"

While it had been annoying that he'd spent so much time chopping wood, it had been nice to look out the window these past two days and watch him work. The play of his muscles beneath his shirt. His big hands gripping the ax handle. Such strength. Stamina.

Maybe she should have come outside sooner.

The idea wound through the back of Lily's mind as North dropped the ax to the ground near his foot and braced his hand atop the handle. Sweat dampened his forehead. His chest heaved with heavy breaths causing his shirt to cling to him.

Lily had never seen any man in Saint Louis who looked like *this*.

North swiped his forearm across his brow. "Let me guess. You want to talk."

Good gracious, he was handsome. The reminder seemed to steal Lily's breath away—and make her forget what she wanted to talk to him about.

He raised an eyebrow. "So you *don't* want to talk?"

She gave herself a mental shake. "Yes. Yes, of course I want to talk."

"Of course..." he grumbled.

Lily straightened her shoulders, forcing herself to concentrate on the matter at hand, rather than the beads of sweat disappearing behind the front of North's shirt.

"It's about Hannah," Lily said, forcing herself to gaze at his face. "She's been gone for two days now. I don't think she's coming back."

North shrugged. "She's busy at the village. She's working."

"Or, she's staying there permanently." Lily shook her head. "Perhaps it's time to give up on the idea of sending her back East."

"No." North picked up the ax again. "Not yet."

"Then when?"

He eyed her sharply. "Are you that anxious to leave this place?"

The question jolted Lily. For months, since shortly after leaving Saint Louis on the wagon train, all she could think of was returning home. But now...

"You're not the same woman who left Saint Louis." North dropped the ax and moved closer to her. "You're different now. This place has changed you. Made you stronger."

A little smile pulled at her lips. "I hadn't thought about it before, but I guess you're right. I've learned a great deal living here. I'm not quite as worthless as I was when I arrived."

North drew nearer. The heat he gave off seemed to change from a warmth brought on by physical work, to something deeper. He cupped her jaw with his palm and gazed into her eyes.

Lily couldn't move. Didn't want to move. Something inside urged her to ease closer. Touch him. Blend with him. Now and forever.

She sensed the same in him. His hand trembled against her cheek, and his eyes darkened. He lowered his head, his lips seeking hers. Lily's heart pounded and she leaned forward.

But he pulled away, a look of pain on his face. North grabbed up the ax and headed toward the forest. Lily watched him walk away, something of herself going along with him.

Then she turned and ran back to the cabin.

The lantern's flickering flame sent shadows wavering across the pages of Lily's journal. She scooted the lantern a little to the left, and began writing again.

Before she'd left on her Western trek, her friend's father, the editor of a Saint Louis newspaper, had asked her to write a series of articles chronicling her journey. Lily had been thrilled at the prospect of having her work published in the newspaper.

The first few weeks of the trip had been uneventful, to say the least. Heavy rains and flooding had delayed their departure. But Lily had managed to fill page after page with her impressions of their preparations, her fellow travelers, and the fear that the delay might be so great as to cancel their trip completely. The window of opportunity for good weather on the Trail was a short one.

But they'd gotten underway, at last. With the Nelson family cooking and cleaning for them, and taking care of the wagon and horses, Lily had wiled away the long days sketching the scenery and filling her journal.

Then her father had injured himself and taken ill. She hadn't written a word since.

Lily paused in her writing and gazed down at the page. She'd decided to begin anew with her journal, though she'd be selective about what she wrote—such as her feelings about North...whatever they were.

The sound of footsteps outside took Lily's attention. Living here beneath the towering trees, she'd become attuned to sounds of birds, animals, in-sects—something she'd rarely noticed back in Saint Louis.

North was still in the forest, no doubt single-handedly attempting to cut a trail through the woods all the way to the Pacific. There'd been no sign of Hannah in days. But the footsteps were light. A woman's steps.

When the cabin door opened and Hannah walked inside, Lily smiled. She'd missed the young girl. North, for whatever reason, seemed to be going out of his way to ignore her. She'd been lonely.

Hannah remained just inside the doorway, waiting to be acknowledged.

"I'm so glad to see you," Lily said, rising from her chair. "Have you been at the village?"

She nodded. "I've been helping with the buffalo. The hunting is good."

"When you left so suddenly the other night, I was afraid something was wrong," Lily said.

Hannah wrinkled her nose and gave a little shud-der. "I don't like Tom Carson."

Lily nodded. "I don't really like him, either. But I do like Grace."

"I like her, too." Hannah ventured a little closer. "I—I liked wearing those clothes. Your clothes. The fancy ones."

"I liked wearing them, too, back in Saint Louis,"

Lily said, smiling at the memory. "I wish there was an occasion for them out here."

A moment passed before Hannah spoke again. "I was thinking while I was at the village. I was thinking that…well, that maybe I could…"

"Wear them again?" Lily asked.

"Yes, but…" Hannah drew in a breath. "Maybe I could do as North asked and go to the East, and tell everyone what it's like to be an Indian."

Lily's eyes widened. She struggled to hold her emotions in check. "Are you sure about this?"

Hannah nodded slowly. From the frown on her face, Lily knew she'd put a great deal of thought into her decision.

"It's a good idea," Hannah said. "It's necessary. And if it will help our people, how can I refuse?"

Lily smiled. "I think you're making the right decision. Let's go tell North."

"I saw him just now in the woods," Hannah said. "I asked him to come in here, but I didn't tell him what I'd decided."

Lily understood that Hannah intended to make North wait as long as possible for her decision. Though she was agreeing to do as he asked and go back East, Hannah still wasn't all that happy with North for presenting her with this difficult decision.

A few minutes later, North came into the cabin. He looked tired and sweaty, his sleeves rolled back, his shirt open in the front. Lily's heart seemed to skip at beat at the sight of him.

"I've decided to do as you asked," Hannah said to him. "I'll travel to the East and teach people there about the Indians."

North nodded slowly and the barest of smiles pulled at his lips. "Good. You'll—"

"Under one condition." Hannah's eyes hardened.

North frowned. "What condition?"

"If I have to learn manners," Hannah told him, "then so do you."

"What?"

"Why should I have to learn all these manners and customs, while you continue to do as you please?" Hannah demanded.

"She has a point," Lily agreed. "As her older brother, I think you should set an example for her."

"But—"

"Besides," Lily pointed out. "How can she possibly learn to be a lady without being in the company of a gentleman?"

"Now listen here—"

"That's my condition." Hannah crossed her arms over her chest, pushed her chin up and glared at her brother. "Take it, or leave it."

Instead of answering, North pointed at Lily. "She's being stubborn and willful. She was never like this before. She learned this from you."

"Me?"

"Eastern ways," he grumbled.

"So are you going along with my condition?" Hannah asked, "or do I go back to the village for good?"

North glared at them both, then stomped outside and slammed the door behind him.

Chapter Fourteen

"Etiquette is associated with rules and regulations, matters of conduct and behavior," Lily announced to her two students seated at the table. Hannah gazed up at her wide eyed; North sat reared back in his chair, his arms folded across his chest.

After much grumbling and grousing, and a few more hours of wood chopping, North had come inside and agreed to participate in Hannah's tutoring.

He wasn't happy.

Lily pressed on with the same speech she remembered Madame DuBois giving at the opening of her deportment classes.

"Etiquette, in its wider and truer sense, does not concern itself with only the details of conduct, but rather with the flowering of that instinct for peace, harmony and good-fellowship. It enhances our social lives, the acts of conduct concerning others, and the small concessions we routinely make to the whims, habits and customs of those around us.''

Lily looked expectantly at her students. ''Any questions so far?''

''Yeah,'' North grumbled. ''Can we eat now?''

Lily had prepared supper, with Hannah's help, and left it warming on the stove. She'd decided that, after a brief overview, instruction on table manners would be the first subject they would tackle.

''We'll eat in a moment. I still need to cover the origin of manners,'' Lily explained, ''as well as the ceremonious aspect of life, the history of customs and traditions—''

''Yeah, okay.'' North pushed up from the table and headed for the stove.

''Fine, then. We'll begin our lesson on table manners while we're eating,'' Lily said, giving in. Engaging in a battle of wills with North, at this point, would do no one any good.

After they'd filled their plates with the stew she'd made and sat down again, Lily opened her one etiquette book that had survived the theft of her other belongings at the fort, and placed it on the table, turning it toward Hannah and North.

''This is a diagram of the proper utensils necessary for a formal supper,'' she said.

Hannah's eyes widened at the array of forks, knives and spoons. ''Oh, my…''

North grunted and started eating.

"But for right now, we'll concentrate on an informal supper." Lily folded her napkins across her lap. "The informal supper hour is so much more than an occasion for eating. It's a time when family and friends gather around the table, not simply to satisfy their hunger, but to enjoy social contact, share experiences of the day, voice opinions—"

"I have an opinion I'd like to share," North said, glancing up from his plate.

Lily ignored him and went on.

"During the informal supper hour, food should be eaten in a leisurely manner," she said. "The atmosphere at the table should be subdued, quiet—"

"Does that mean you're going to stop talking now?" North asked.

Lily narrowed her eyes at him. "You are not being helpful."

"Yeah, well—"

"You said you'd cooperate," Lily reminded him.

North pointed at the utensil diagram. "Eastern men actually put up with all this?"

"Yes, of course they do."

"Hell, they must be better trained than my horses." North picked up his plate, rose from the table and stalked outside.

The air, the heat seemed to leave the cabin with North. Lily eased back in her chair, acutely aware of the emptiness his departure created.

She turned to Hannah. "I don't think we can count on your brother to sit through anymore etiquette lessons."

"I know. I just wanted to annoy him as much as possible." Hannah nodded toward the book. "Explain what all those things are used for, will you?"

Lily blew out a heavy breath as she crossed the yard toward the barn. Her back ached slightly and her head seemed a little fuzzy. Two and a half days of table manners had taken its toll on her—and her pupil.

"North?" Lily called as she approached the barn.

She stopped in the open doorway and gazed inside. The afternoon sun was cooled considerably by the trees that sheltered the cabin; the barn was just as comfortable. She liked the rich, earthy smells of horses and leather…and North.

He looked up from the harness he'd been working on, set it aside and walked over.

"How're the lessons going?" he asked, and nodded toward the cabin.

"Fine. Just fine."

North looked at her in that way he had of demanding—without a word—that she tell him what was really on her mind.

Lily's shoulders slumped. "I'm worn-out," she confessed. She didn't tell him, though, that in this state of mind, she'd wanted to come to him. Be near him. Soak up his strength. Be fortified by his gentle calm. She didn't tell him that, though, because she didn't understand it herself.

"What about Hannah?" North asked. "How is she holding up?"

"I sent her back to the village for a while," Lily admitted. "She needed a respite from instructions. We've covered the use of the knife, fork, spoon and napkin. The handling of stemware. Proper posture at the table, appropriate manners. Next, we'll move on to the afternoon tea, the casual tea, the formal tea. Then, the formal luncheon, informal luncheon, supper, buffet service and breakfast."

North shook his head in amazement. "Do you miss all that?"

Lily drew in a breath and let it out slowly. "Actually, I wonder now why it seemed so important that I learn it in the first place. I wish, sometimes, that I could go back and do it all differently."

"Why?"

"Because all that schooling kept me from my father, the last of my family. And for what purpose?" Lily shook her head. "Now, simply sitting around a table with people I care about seems wonderful, regardless of which fork should be used with which food."

"People you care about?" North asked. "Do you mean your aunt in Richmond?"

The notion startled Lily because Aunt Maribel

hadn't been on her mind when she'd told him that. And now that she really thought about it, Lily wasn't sure who she pictured seated around her imaginary supper table.

North tensed and his gaze darted across the yard. He stepped in front of Lily, blocking her from whatever had taken his attention.

She leaned around him and saw a figure traipsing through the woods toward the cabin. Afternoon shadows camouflaged the person for another moment, then Lily saw that it was Grace Carson. A few more seconds passed before she realized that Tom wasn't with her.

Grace didn't wait to be acknowledged, as was the custom. She hurried forward. As she drew near, Lily saw that she was out of breath and disheveled. Lily exchanged a troubled look with North and they went to meet Grace.

"What's wrong?" Lily asked, taking her hand.

"Nothing." She glanced behind her. "Nothing."

"You're out of breath and—"

"I'm fine…fine." Grace pushed away a lock of hair that had come loose. "I—I just came by for a—a quick visit, that's all."

North touched her chin and turned her face toward him. A purple bruise marred her cheek.

She pulled away. "It's nothing. Really. I—I fell. That's all. It was an accident." Grace turned to Lily.

"Can I speak with you? Please? In—in private? It won't take long."

Lily shared yet another troubled look with North, then said, "Yes, of course, Grace. Come inside."

Grace glanced toward the woods again, then hurried into the cabin. When Lily followed her inside, Grace latched on to her forearm with a desperate strength.

"When are you leaving? When? How soon?" she demanded.

"Just as soon as Hannah's instruction is completed," Lily said. "Grace, what is it? What's wrong? Why are you—"

"You must take me with you," she begged. "You must. Please, say that you will. Please!"

"Sit down, Grace, tell me—"

"I have to get away from this place. I have to. I hate it here." Grace's hands trembled.

"Your husband—"

"Tom won't let me leave. When we came here last spring he said it would be only for a few months. Then he wouldn't leave. He won't let *me* leave." Tears sprang to her eyes as her words rushed out. "I've written to my family, but I'm sure he's destroyed my letters. I haven't heard a word from any of them since we got here. He seldom lets me go to the fort—or anywhere."

Horrified, Lily said, "Grace, that's terrible. Please, sit down and—"

"I can't. Tom's hunting today—at least, he said he was hunting. I don't know. I'm afraid he went to the fort and is involved with—" Grace shook her head frantically. "If he finds out I've come over here… Please, Lily, promise me that you'll take me with you when you go. It's my only chance to escape this place."

"Yes, of course, Grace. Of course, you can go. But how will you manage it?"

"I'll sneak away, somehow. I'll do something. Anything. I can't live in this place any longer." Grace gulped a breath of air. "You're leaving soon. You'll have to."

"I don't know for sure when I'll go. It depends on Hannah's instruction. North said he'd take—"

"If you don't leave soon, it will be too late," Grace told her. "Too late in the year."

Lily gasped. "What?"

"The weather will make the Trail too dangerous," Grace said. "If you don't leave soon, you'll have to spend the winter here."

"The winter…?" Lily's thoughts spun. Spend the winter? Here?

She should have thought of that possibility already, she realized. Their departure from Saint Louis had been carefully timed. The return could be no different.

Another thought slipped into her mind. Why hadn't North mentioned that to her? Had he figured she already knew? Did he think it was unnecessary to point it out to her?

Or was he deliberately deceiving her?

Nothing was more important to North than for his plan for Hannah to come to fruition. Lily had fought him on it, Hannah had done the same, but he'd clung to it determinedly. He was adamant about helping his people.

But at Lily's expense?

Ugly memories presented themselves. Her father hadn't told her the truth about his business affairs, his financial problems, the real reason he wanted to come West. He'd kept it from her—all of it. She'd based her decision to come with him on what was in her heart, rather than the facts as Augustus knew them.

The men at Bent's Fort had been no less deceptive. In fact, the only truly kind person she'd met there was Jacob Tanner, who'd brought her meal trays. Every other man in the place had been out for himself—at her expense.

Including North, she realized. He'd settled her debts to serve his own purpose, not out of the goodness of his heart.

"Don't worry," Lily said to Grace. "I'm leaving this place in plenty of time to make it to my aunt's home in Richmond before the winter. You're coming with me. I won't go without you."

"Promise," Grace insisted. "Please, promise me that we'll go together."

"I promise," Lily said solemnly.

"Thank you." Grace squeezed her eyes closed for a second, fighting back a rush of tears. "I have to get back to the cabin before Tom realizes—"

"Of course. Run along."

Grace started toward the door, then turned back. "You won't tell Tom I was here, will you? I mean, if he should come by and—"

"I won't mention it."

Grace glanced outside. "What about North? Will he tell Tom—"

Lily shook her head. "Don't worry. I'll be sure that he doesn't."

"Thank you," Grace said, and dashed out the door.

Lily walked outside and watched as Grace melted into the forest. When she turned to go back inside, she found North behind her. Lily gasped, still unaccustomed to his silent approach.

"What's wrong with Grace?" he asked and nodded toward the forest.

Lily pressed her lips together, fighting off the familiar urge to tell North the truth.

"She doesn't want her husband to know...just yet," Lily said. "We must respect her privacy."

"Sure," North agreed.

"Grace wanted to ask me about something...personal,'' Lily lied. ''She asked me because there isn't another woman around.''

The vague mention of a womanly health problem was enough to send North on his way without further questions. Lily was glad. She didn't really want to lie to him. But she couldn't tell him the truth, either.

Because deep in her heart, she didn't trust him.

Chapter Fifteen

He'd chopped wood—more wood than he'd need this winter. He'd endured vivid dreams and sleepless nights.

All because of Lily.

North stood outside the barn gazing eastward toward the rising sun. The treetops shimmered in the day's first golden rays and rustled with the gentle breeze.

This quiet, solitary time before the forest came alive had always brought him peace. Cleared his head, focused his thoughts.

But today, as with so many days lately, North's mind was anything but focused—except on one thing.

Lily.

Drawing in a cleansing breath of crisp morning air, North shifted his gaze to the cabin. She was inside still sleeping, probably. Bad enough that she'd turned his home upside down with her Eastern ways. She also affected his thoughts, his actions… and his heart.

For a long time now, North had known that his destiny lay with his vision to bring peace between the Indians and the white settlers. Every man on this earth had a purpose, and he'd found his.

But Lily had come with it, and now…

North turned sharply and headed toward the barn. He'd wrestled with the problem of finding a way to help his people for a long time. He'd come up with the idea, then gained Lily and Hannah's cooperation.

Yet now that his plan was underway, he still found no harmony in his life. Because it meant that once Hannah was ready, Lily would leave.

He'd tried to fight off his feelings for Lily, but the woman simply would not leave his thoughts.

Now, there was only one thing he could do.

"I'm going to the village," North said, walking through the cabin door.

Lily looked up from the stove and the eggs she was frying. While North wasn't much for conversation, he'd never greeted her in this fashion first thing in the morning. He sounded troubled, displeased, or angry, perhaps. She didn't know why.

"If you're going to the village to bring Hannah back," Lily said, "I told her that she could stay there for a day or so. It was my idea."

North shook his head. "No, this has nothing to do with Hannah."

"You're going there to trade horses?"

"No, I—I just need to go."

"Oh." Lily studied him as he shifted his weight from one foot to the other. He wouldn't meet her eyes.

Obviously, he didn't want to tell her his reasons for going to the village. Though it didn't suit her, she couldn't make him do something he didn't want to do. She had no right to expect it.

But she didn't want to spend the day at the cabin all alone. The hours dragged, and despite his contention that she had nothing to fear, she was, in fact, frightened here alone.

"Can I go with you?" Lily asked, the idea suddenly coming to her.

North's gaze came up quickly and landed on her. He drew back a little—whether from her or her suggestion, she didn't know.

"I'd like to see the village and meet your friends," she said.

He tilted his head the way she'd seen him do so many times before when he was about to disagree with her. Lily rushed ahead.

"If I go, if I see the village and the Cheyenne firsthand, I'll be able to talk to people back East and explain the Indian ways, just as you want Hannah to do," she said. "That's what you want, isn't it?"

"Yes, but—"

"But what?"

"It's just that…"

"What?"

North fumed silently for a moment. Lily sensed that he still didn't want her to go, but wasn't going to give her a specific reason.

He looked hard at her, and just that quickly, she saw his mind change, as if something had occurred to him suddenly.

"You can go," North said. "It would be a good idea if you did."

She didn't know what he was alluding to, but didn't care, either. All that mattered was that she wouldn't have to spend the day alone here at the cabin.

When they finished breakfast, North rose from the table, told her to fill the canteens and pack some food, then went outside.

Lily made quick work of cleaning up the breakfast dishes, then did as he'd asked and filled the canteens from the water bucket and put bread, cheese and apples in a sack.

Excitement warmed her at the prospect of leaving. She realized she hadn't been farther than a few hundred yards from the cabin since she'd arrived here.

Grace Carson filled her mind. How long since she'd been anywhere? Lily wondered.

But when Lily stepped outside the cabin, her enthusiasm for the excursion cooled considerably when she saw North leading two horses over.

"We're…riding to the village?" she asked, hearing the disappointment in her voice.

North tied the horses to the hitching rail. "Don't you know how to ride?"

"Well, yes, of course I ride," Lily told him. "But, well, don't you have a sidesaddle?"

"No," he said, as if it were the strangest question he'd ever heard.

Lily knew the village was close, since Hannah hiked back and forth so often.

"Can't we walk?" she asked.

His expression soured. "Horse traders don't walk."

"And ladies don't ride astride."

North looked her up and down, bringing a flush to Lily's cheeks. "Why not?"

She fought off her embarrassment. "Because it's not considered ladylike."

He sighed, as if he understood her words but didn't necessarily agree with the concept, and said, "Then you'll have to stay here."

North took the food sack and canteen from her hands and tied them to the saddle of one of the horses.

"No, wait," Lily insisted. She couldn't spend a day here alone—she simply couldn't.

Good manners be damned, she decided. Lily went

to the other horse, put her foot in the stirrup and pulled herself into the saddle. Her skirt and petticoats billowed around her. She pressed them down, covering as much of her legs as possible.

"You sure you know what you're doing?" North asked, handing the reins up to her.

"Do try to keep up," she said crisply, and off she went.

He caught her by the time they reached the woods, which was just as well, since Lily didn't have the foggiest idea where the Cheyenne village was located. She hadn't a prayer of outriding North, and she knew it. Horsemanship among the Indians was legendary. Riding bareback, using both hands to bring down a buffalo with bow and arrow, was common.

North rode at her side, keeping an eye on her. Lily guessed he wasn't convinced that she knew how to ride. Yet she took little comfort in his nearness, with her skirts flapping in the breeze and her ankles showing.

Madame DuBois would faint dead away if she could see her now.

There was no trail that Lily could detect through the trees, yet North seemed to know exactly how far to ride in which direction, which way to turn. She wondered if they'd come near Bent's Fort, but quickly realized they rode in the opposite direction.

At the top of a ridge, North pulled his horse to a

stop. Lily drew up alongside him and stopped as well. Below, in a clearing, was the Cheyenne village.

Tepees were arranged in several circles, one within another. Even from this distance, Lily saw that the exteriors were decorated with colorful symbols. Smoke rose from the campfires that burned in the village.

For as long as Lily could remember, the Indians had been spoken of as savages, never to be trusted. Eastern newspapers carried accounts of the atrocities they committed. Travelers on the wagon train had feared Indian attacks above all else. Yet the village, nestled cozy in the valley, looked peaceful.

"Do you want to go back to the cabin?" North asked, seeming to sense her unease.

"No," Lily answered without hesitation.

"Afraid?" he asked.

She looked at him. "A little," she admitted.

"Don't worry," North said. "The Cheyenne only dine on the flesh of white women during medicine ceremonies."

Lily gasped, then saw the little grin lurking around North's mouth.

"I don't suppose there's a medicine ceremony scheduled for today?" she asked.

His grin grew a little wider. "No, not today."

"Then let's go."

She urged her horse forward and followed him down to the village.

Cook pots hung over campfires, filling the air with delicious aromas. Young, dark-haired children dressed in buckskins ran between the tepees. Dogs barked. Women moved about the village, some tending the cooking, some sewing and weaving baskets, others hard at work at chores Lily didn't recognize.

Everyone paused in their work, turned and stared, as Lily rode at North's side.

When they stopped the horses and dismounted, Lily's stomach tingled much as it had when she'd lived in Saint Louis and walked into a party, knowing that she was being watched, judged. Yet here she wasn't offended by the attention she'd garnered.

North took the reins from her and stepped close. "They don't see too many white women here."

Lily drew herself up and straightened her shoulders. "No doubt they've heard how strong and intimidating we can be," she said softly.

North chuckled. "Hannah will show you around the village."

"Where will you be?" Lily asked. For weeks she'd lived with him at the cabin, always knowing he was close by, and the thought of being parted from him now caused an emptiness to well in the pit of her stomach.

"I won't be far," he promised, and led the horses away.

Lily fought the urge to go after him—but not because she was in a strange place, surrounded by people she didn't know. It was something else. Something deeper. Just what, she couldn't name.

Hannah appeared just as North left. "Why are
you here?" she asked, not unkindly.

"North wanted to come, and I didn't want to stay
at the cabin alone."

Hannah watched her brother as he and the horses
moved through the maze of tepees. "He's troubled.
He comes here when he's troubled."

"Do you think so?" Lily asked, turning back,
catching a last look at him. "About what?"

"It's not for me to say," Hannah told her. "Come
with me. I'll show you the village."

Lily walked with Hannah as the young girl explained the workings of the tribe.

"We're hunters," Hannah said. "We follow the
buffalo. Our scouts watch the herd and alert the village when it's on the move. Within hours, the village is dismantled, packed and we're on the march."

"All of this?" Lily asked gazing around in
amazement. "Everything is packed and moved?"

"All that we own is designed to move easily and
quickly," Hannah said. "The women take down the
tepees, then put them up again when a new site is
selected."

"Oh, my…" Lily shook her head. The women of

the tribe did all this? By themselves? No wonder North had thought her so useless.

"Do you like living here?" she asked Hannah as they walked.

"It's my home," Hannah said.

"But not North's. He left the village, built a cabin for himself. He trades with the settlers."

"North is a brave and cunning warrior. He proved himself worthy of his Cheyenne blood many times," Hannah told her, pride evident in her voice. "But he answered the call of our English ancestors, choosing for himself a permanent home and a different sort of life. He dishonors no one with his decision."

The tribal women eyed Lily cautiously as she and Hannah stopped to watch them.

"I have to help with the hides," Hannah told Lily.

She eyed the Cheyenne women, hard at work.

"Can I help, too?" she asked.

Hannah hesitated for a moment, as if not sure whether it was a good idea. Then, finally, she spoke to the women in their native tongue. One of them answered, but Lily couldn't tell from her tone whether or not she was receptive to the offer. The woman pointed at Lily's dress, then several other women spoke as well.

"You can help," Hannah said to Lily. "But there's something you must do first."

"What?" Lily asked, throwing a nervous glance at the women.

"Come with me." Hannah took her hand.

"But—"

"Come on," she insisted, and pulled her away.

The visit to the village had seemed a good idea this morning, North thought as he sat beneath the towering trees in the hills above the settlement. In fact, it had seemed like the only thing he could do, under the circumstances.

And now, he'd proven himself right. But for a very different reason.

A reason that, somehow, left him feeling empty inside.

For hours today, he'd sat with the men of the tribe and talked about the hunt, the settlers, the traders at the fort; even the Cheyenne had heard the rumor about the army's Western expedition. He'd caught up on the news at the village.

Then he'd hiked to this spot on the hill where the entire village was spread out below him, and made himself comfortable, sipping from the canteen Lily had filled for them.

When she'd asked to come with him this morning, he'd told her no. North needed this time to himself, to talk to his friends here, sort through the problems that had plagued him lately.

But standing in his cabin this morning, watching

her at the stove, he'd decided that Lily should come
with him. It would decide things for him, one way
or the other. Because if he saw Lily here at the village, so very far out of her element, he'd know once
and for all that she didn't belong here.

And he could let her go.

North sipped from the canteen as he watched the
women of the village going about the routine of their
day. Working, caring for the children, cooking,
cleaning, tending to their many chores.

No sign of Lily.

She'd be easy to spot. No doubt about it. The only
woman covered from ankle to wrist to throat in a
dress of soft, flowing fabric. Ruffled white petticoats. Hair secured atop her head.

He'd watched for hours now and had not seen her.
Not once. He could only guess where she was. In a
tepee crying? Begging someone to find him so he
could take her back to the cabin? Hiding in the
woods somewhere, frightened by something that
didn't even exist?

From his vantage point on the hill, North could
see the horse she'd ridden today and knew she
hadn't gone home on her own.

A thread of worry wound through his thoughts.
Surely by now she knew enough not to attempt to
hike through the woods alone.

North opened the food sack Lily had prepared.

Inside he saw bread, a wedge of cheese and apples. His heart tumbled. She'd also packed two napkins.

Napkins.

North clenched one of them in his fist as he pulled it from the sack. Soft fabric. Colorful. Made from one of her own dresses. He lifted it to his face and drew in a deep breath. It smelled of Lily.

North turned his gaze to the village once more. Carefully, he scrutinized every woman he saw.

Where was Lily? Why couldn't—why wouldn't—she grab hold of the life here?

She'd been almost completely helpless when he'd first seen her at the fort, and when she'd foolishly wandered into the prairie alone. But she'd learned so much since then, showed him a strength he hadn't imagined.

He'd brought her with him to the village today to prove to himself that she didn't belong here in this life. Yet disappointment settled in the pit of his belly as he realized that was true.

North shoved the napkin into the sack and got to his feet. So now he knew, knew for sure. It couldn't be more obvious that Lily didn't belong here. And no matter how his heart ached at the realization, he knew he had to accept that fact and let her go.

North wound his way down the hillside to the village. The day was growing late. They would have to head back to the cabin soon.

"You are troubled," a man said.

North turned and saw Running Wolf seated outside his tepee. The man had been a friend of North's father for as long as North could remember, and was thought of among the tribe as a wise man. Now, the many winters of his life showed on his once strong face. His movements were slowed by age. Running Wolf wouldn't likely see the spring.

North sat down beside him on the mat in front of his tepee, not at all surprised the older man had sensed his problem.

"Yes," North admitted with a heavy sigh. "I've got a problem or two."

Running Wolf didn't answer. His gaze drifted to the distant horizon.

"I thought I understood my future. I thought I had it figured out," North said. "But I guess I was wrong."

Running Wolf offered no response.

"What I want," North began, "that is, the woman that I want…well, she can't be mine."

Minutes slipped by while Running Wolf continued to stare at the horizon. Heaviness settled around North's heart. For a brief moment, he'd hoped that his wise friend could give him some advice that would make him feel better. Now, it seemed he'd expected too much of the old man.

North rose only to have Running Wolf raise his hand, stopping him.

"Your future isn't cloudy," the man said, as if

he saw something in the distance that no one else could interpret. "You will have the woman you desire."

North's heart lurched. "But which woman? Someone I know now, or—"

"And many children," Running Wolf said. "In a place called Colorado."

"Colorado…?"

North waited, hoping Running Wolf would speak again, but the old man closed his eyes. His head slumped forward until his chin rested against his chest. North left him.

So he was destined to marry, if Running Wolf could be believed. North walked through the village, his heart heavier than when he'd awakened this morning.

If his future wife couldn't be Lily—and he didn't see how it could be, given that she couldn't possibly thrive in a life with him here—then who would it be? North gazed at the tribal women as he walked. One of them? he wondered. A woman he'd yet to meet? Someone who—

North jerked to a stop at the sight of Lily on the ground beside the fire. His heart rose in his throat.

What had happened to her?

Chapter Sixteen

North stared, unable to move, at the sight of Lily seated on the ground around the cook fire with Hannah and a half-dozen other women. He could hardly believe his eyes. No wonder he hadn't spotted her from the hills. He barely recognized her now.

Lily wore a doeskin dress, the soft fabric hugging her curves, barely covering her knees. She had on moccasins. Her hair hung in two long braids, almost to her waist. She chatted with Hannah and the other women as she dipped flat bread into the common cook pot, eating stew in the Cheyenne tradition.

The women quieted when one of them spotted North. They all looked toward him.

To his further surprise, Lily didn't offer him the smile he usually saw on her face. Instead, her expression grew serious and she got quickly to her feet.

She held out her right palm level with her shoulder and moved her hand sharply downward. *Stop.*

North stopped.

Then she held her hand, palm up, against her stomach and moved it right to left. *Hungry.*

North felt a smile bloom across his face as his belly warmed—but not because of her proffered stew.

He extended his right index finger and swept it toward his face. *Come.*

The women giggled and Hannah looked on with pride as Lily walked away with him.

"How did you learn—"

"Hannah taught me," Lily said, a big smile on her face, her words coming out in an excited rush. "She and the other women are so nice. They let me help with the hides. They showed me what to do and, of course, the smell was terrible and I wasn't very good at it, but they were patient, except for that one woman who pinched my arm when I didn't do it right, but I learned really quickly."

At the edge of the village, they stopped under the canopy of tall trees. North touched the doeskin sleeve of her dress.

"And this?"

Lily blushed and ran her hands down her skirt. "The women said my own dress would get in the way, so Hannah gave me this to wear."

North looked her up and down. "It's nice."

"It's scandalous." Lily touched her palms to her cheeks and giggled. "Madame DuBois would have an absolute fit if she was to see me in it. But it's very comfortable. I can see why the women here dress the way they do."

"You look…" North couldn't find the words to express how beautiful she looked, or the joy that filled his heart. So he kissed her.

North pulled her against him and locked her in his embrace, then covered her mouth with his. Stunned, Lily stiffened for a brief second, then relaxed against him. He blended his lips against her, tasting her, wanting her—all of her.

His blood burned hot for her, and he wanted more. But instead he broke off their kiss and leaned his forehead against hers, still craving her touch.

"Beautiful," he whispered. "You look beautiful."

Lily curled her arms around his neck. "Hannah asked if we were staying here tonight."

"Do you want to go home?" North asked.

"I like the village and the people. I'd like to spend the night, if it's all right with you."

"We'll stay," North told her, the urge to do anything that pleased her nearly overwhelming him.

Reluctantly, he let her go, and they returned to the village.

Lily didn't see North again. She worked alongside Hannah and the other women cooking, cleaning, then went into one of the tepees as the sky grew dark.

The tepee was larger than Lily expected, a height greater than the high ceilings of her father's Saint Louis home. Since it was summer the hides that were usually pegged to the ground for warmth were rolled up, letting in the cool night breeze. Hannah gave her a woven mat to sleep on. Lily undressed and stretched out on it wearing her chemise and pantalets.

Staring into the darkness, Lily listened to the sounds of the village fade into the night. She relaxed, tired from the hard day's work, but exhilarated by the things she'd learned and seen today.

Not the least of which was North's kiss.

The warmth in her belly deepened at the memory of him taking her into his arms, holding her, kissing her. The strength of his arms, the hardness of his body.

He belonged here in this wild land. She'd thought that the moment she saw him at the fort. Yet now, the land didn't seem quite so untamed. And she didn't feel quite so out of place.

Minutes passed and Lily heard the heavy breathing of Hannah and the two other women who shared the tepee as they fell asleep. Lily closed her eyes.

They popped open later—she didn't know how

much later—at the feel of something on her arm. She tried to rise, but a hand pressed her down.

"Shh."

Lily squinted into the darkness and saw North beside her. "What are you—"

"Come with me," he whispered. "There's something I want you to see."

"But—"

North slipped silently out of the tepee.

Lily found her dress where she'd left it earlier in the day and pulled it on, not bothering with her petticoats. She'd needed Hannah's help to get into the doeskin dress, and couldn't manage it in the dark by herself. She'd taken her hair out of its braids when she'd lain down and didn't want to take time to put it up again, so she left it loose around her shoulders. Pulling on the moccasins, Lily closed the front fasteners of her dress and ducked out of the tepee into the night.

North waited nearby. He touched his fingers to his lips; she didn't need to understand sign language to know he wanted her to be quiet.

Then he held out his hand. Lily didn't hesitate. She took it and he led her through the village and into the forest.

"I want to show you something," North said as they made their way through the trees.

There was no moon, but North didn't seem to need any light to find his way. Lily clung to his hand, his big, warm fingers firm and reassuring around hers.

After a few minutes, she heard the sound of a rushing stream. They pressed on through the trees and finally North stopped at the edge of a clearing.

"This is a favorite spot of mine," North said.

Even though her eyes had adjusted to the darkness, Lily still could see very little.

"Be patient," North said, and sat down, pulling her down beside him.

The grass was soft and cool beneath Lily as she drew her legs sideways and tucked her skirt over them. Though she'd walked around the village in her doeskin dress today with her calves showing for the very first time in her adult life, it still felt odd to do the same in her gown.

Gradually, the distant horizon brightened and the moon rose. Its beams lit the forest, then reflected off the still waters of the small lake that had been hidden by the darkness.

"It's easy to see why you like it here," Lily said, quietly.

"It's beautiful. Like you." North turned to her. "I come here sometimes when I have a problem, when I need to think."

"What are you thinking about now?" Lily wanted to know.

He shifted closer until his arm brushed hers. Heat

rolled off him, penetrating the fabric of her sleeve, finding its way to her belly, somehow.

"I was thinking about how you've surprised me," North told her. He smiled. "You're a strong woman, Miss Lily St. Claire."

She gave him a saucy grin. "I think I worked as hard as any Cheyenne woman today. In fact, I think I should have a Cheyenne name."

"Names are chosen at birth, but often changed to represent the person once they become an adult," North explained.

Lily nodded thoughtfully. "So what name do you think I should have?"

North made a show of settling back, furrowing his brow and studying her for a moment. "Let's see…how about Long Talker?"

"Long Talker!" she exclaimed.

"Or maybe Many Words." North snapped his fingers. "I know. We'll call you Little Yapping Dog."

"Oh, you." Lily swatted him on the arm. North chuckled, the sound rumbling in the quiet night.

"So, is there a problem that brings you to your favorite spot tonight?" Lily asked.

"Yes," North said. "You."

"Me? I'm a problem?"

"You make me weak."

"Weak?" she asked. Never in her life would she describe North as weak. "How could I—"

"Weak with desire." He edged closer. She felt his breath against her face. "Desire for…you."

North kissed her. He cupped his hand against the back of her head and eased her down onto the ground. His lips moved against hers, seeking, tasting, devouring.

He pushed himself up on his elbow and raised his head, his breath heavy. He traced his fingers down the curve of her jaw.

"Surely you know how much I want you."

Lily's stomach fluttered. "No…"

His brows raised. "After all that firewood I chopped? Did you think I was doing that because we needed it?"

Lily smiled, a new warmth winding its way through her, settling around her heart.

She looped her arms around his neck, gazing up into his eyes. "I admit, I've had some… unladylike…thoughts about you, too."

North grinned and shifted closer, bringing his body against hers. "Such as?"

"Your chest," she whispered, unable to bring herself to say the words aloud. Lily touched her fingertip against his bare flesh at the top of his shirt. "I wondered what it felt like."

North plucked open the buttons of his shirt and long johns with no hesitation. His bare skin shone in the moonlight, his chest slick and muscular.

"Can I touch—"

"Oh, yes…" North moaned.

Lily laid her palm against his chest. He groaned deep in his throat, then kissed her again. His mouth moved over hers with a new depth, a new want. The heat he gave off wrapped itself around Lily, drew her closer. She kissed him back.

His hand traveled down her shoulder and cupped her breast. Lily gasped, but didn't pull away. Somehow, she couldn't. She didn't want to. The buttons of her dress gave way slowly and she felt the rush of night air against her flesh for an instant, before North's big, hot palm covered her.

He leaned down, kissing a trail from her throat to her breasts. Lily gasped at the feel of his tongue caressing her intimately, then gasped once more as he shifted closer, bringing the hard length of him against her thigh.

The exquisite delight he showed her made Lily anxious to return the favor. She pushed her hand inside his shirt, touching him in the same way. North groaned.

Lily's breath came quicker, leaving her slightly dizzy. Her thoughts evaporated under the touch of his hands and the sensations he elicited from her. Never had anything felt so right to her.

Then, without warning, North lifted his head and withdrew his hand.

"We…we have to stop," he whispered, his words

desperate and urgent. Heat rolled from him. "Now…or I won't be able to stop."

The cool air against her heated skin brought back Lily's good sense. She realized what he was saying…what he was asking.

Her cheeks flushed, yet she wasn't embarrassed. Nothing in her life had ever seemed so right. But was she ready for what lay ahead?

North didn't give her a chance to decide. He tugged her chemise into place and pulled her dress closed, then sat up. Lily fastened her buttons and sat up, as well.

The moon had risen high above the horizon now, its beams shimmering across the silvery lake. They sat side by side for a while in silence.

"We should go back to the village," North said with some effort. He turned to her. "Shouldn't we?"

Lily hesitated. "We should…I suppose."

Another long moment dragged by while they looked at each other.

"We should," North finally said.

He rose, offered his hand, then walked with her back to her tepee. A long, tense moment passed while he just looked at her, and Lily wondered if he would sweep her into his arms and carry her back to the lake.

He didn't. He left without a word.

Hours passed, but Lily couldn't sleep. She finally

dozed off as dawn's light filtered into the tepee. She dressed in her familiar gown, put up her hair and went outside to find North waiting with the horses.

After a few words with Hannah, Lily mounted up and they rode back to the cabin. North still didn't speak. But he wasn't angry. She sensed no hostility from him. It was more an internal struggle to keep himself in check.

When they reached the barn, Lily lingered as North tended to the horses. They walked to the cabin together, stopped, and eyed the closed door.

The place had never seemed so isolated to Lily. They were alone together in the vast wilderness. Just the two of them.

North's gaze burned into her. The heat washed over her, kindling the embers he'd awakened in her last night.

"Lily…" He said her name aloud; his tone, his expression seemed more a plea.

Her heart raced. "I told Hannah not to come back until tomorrow."

His expression darkened. Want and need seemed to spread outward from him, covering her like a warm blanket.

"Lily, I—"

North swept her against him and took her mouth with his. Lily threw her arms around his neck and rose on her toes, kissing him with a fervor she'd never known.

With one arm around her waist, North reached backward and opened the cabin door. He pulled her inside, never breaking their kiss, then kicked the door closed. Arms entwined, they kissed until North lifted his head.

"Are you sure?" he whispered, his voice raspy. He drew away slightly. "We can stop—"

"No," Lily said quickly. "I'm sure."

He kissed her once more, this time capturing her waist with both hands and pulling her full against him. He groaned with pleasure.

Lily's knees trembled, caught in the strange but pleasurable sensations swirling through her. She glanced toward the bunk in the corner—

And screamed.

A man was in her bed.

Chapter Seventeen

Lily's bloodcurdling scream brought the man fully awake, tangled in the buffalo robes, hair sticking out, wild-eyed and, apparently, as frightened as she.

North stepped in front of her, sheltering her, towering over the bunk.

"Lordy day, I don't mean no harm," the man shouted, cowering, holding both arms over his head to protect himself. "I didn't hurt nothing. And I didn't take nothing, either—I swear!"

The man's plea prodded Lily's memory. The voice was familiar. She'd heard it before, she was sure of it. But where?

She stepped alongside North and took a good look at the man.

He was young, she realized, thin, disheveled, wearing long johns with patched elbows and trousers that were at least a size too big.

"Jacob?" she ventured. "Jacob Tanner?"

"Yes, ma'am, it's me, all right." He cast a fearful glance at North, and slowly lowered his hands. "From the fort, ma'am. Remember? I had a job helping out in the kitchen. I fetched meals for you and your papa back when he was sick."

North relaxed his stance only marginally and scowled down at Jacob, as if the young man's explanation still left him suspicious.

"What on earth are you doing here?" Lily asked, gesturing with her hands to encompass the cabin. "Did something happen at the fort?"

"Yes, ma'am, Miss Lily, I reckon you could say that, all right. I've had myself a patch of bad luck, that's for dang sure. Real bad luck. About the worst luck I can remember." Jacob struggled to untangle himself from the buffalo robes and got to his feet. "Not that any of it was my fault, I want you to know."

"Tell us what happened," Lily said, her shock and curiosity at finding him here in the cabin transforming into a simmering fear at hearing he'd run into trouble at the fort.

Jacob hiked up his sagging trousers and looped the suspenders over his shoulders. He smoothed down his spiked hair, looking once more at North.

"I hope you don't think ill of me, barging in like this," Jacob said and ducked his head apologetically. "But there wasn't nobody around yesterday when I got here, and I'd been out on the prairie for a while by then, and I just couldn't walk no farther, and I had no place else to go, things being what they was."

"Okay, fine. Leave now." North grasped his forearm and pulled him toward the door.

Lily gasped. "Good gracious, North, we can't just toss him out."

North glowered at Jacob for a moment, as if he didn't see anything wrong with doing just that, then released his arm.

"I'll pay you for my lodging and for the food I ate," Jacob promised, rubbing his arm absently. "'Course now, I've got no cash money, exactly. But I can work for you. I can do just about anything you might want me to do. Haul water, cook, chop wood."

"Looks like I'll be doing the wood chopping around here…*again,*" North grumbled and plopped down on the kitchen chair.

Lily flushed, suddenly understanding why North was so anxious to get rid of Jacob. She pushed on, hoping the young man didn't realize what he'd interrupted or pick up on their distress.

"What are you doing out here?" Lily asked. "Why aren't you at the fort? What happened?"

"It was downright ugly, I can tell you that, Miss Lily," Jacob said, as he stuck his foot into his boot and tugged it on. "I don't know what's got into those fellas. I swear, I just don't know."

"What fellas? Hiram Fredericks and his… friends?" Lily asked, but she was sure she already knew what the answer would be.

"Yes, ma'am." Jacob pulled on his other boot. "Mr. Fredericks and some of the men took it in their heads that I was passing along information to the army about that expedition everybody's so up in arms about."

"You?" Lily exclaimed, unable to keep the surprise from her voice.

"Yes, ma'am," Jacob said, and flapped his arms against his side, as if he didn't understand it either. "One of the cooks, he overheard them saying they was coming after me, so he came back to the kitchen and told me. So I took off out of there. Just took off."

"You left the fort alone, on foot? Without any provisions?" Lily asked. Jacob must have indeed been frightened to do such a reckless thing. He'd lived at the fort long enough to know what could happen to a man alone on the prairie, with no supplies.

"It was either that or answer to Mr. Fredericks." Jacob shook his head. "The way they was talking, I was scared for my life. I don't know for sure, but I think they would've killed me."

Lily glanced back at North still seated in the chair. His arms were crossed over his chest and his ex-

pression was impassive. She wasn't sure if he was
upset about Jacob's ordeal…or Jacob's presence.

"Are their accusations true?" Lily asked. She
couldn't imagine that they would be. Jacob hardly
seemed the type of young man to carry on clandes-
tine activities, but she had to ask, had to know.
"Were you passing on information to the army?"

"Shoot, no," Jacob declared. He shook his head
so hard his bangs fell over his forehead. "Why, I
got better sense than to do something like that. Anybody who'd get involved with that is just asking for
trouble."

A moment passed in silence. Finally Lily said,
"So what are you going to do?"

"Dang if I know," Jacob said, looking genuinely
perplexed. "I took off from the fort so quick I
couldn't bring nothing with me, not even the little
bit of money I'd saved up from my job." He turned
to North. "Would it be all right if I stayed here for
another couple of days or so, just until I figure something out?"

North glared at him.

"I won't cause a problem," Jacob promised.

"You've already caused a problem," North
grumbled. He pushed himself out of the chair and
took a minute to give Jacob a long, hard look.

Lily almost spoke up for North and gave permission for Jacob to stay, fearing that North was about

to refuse him. She couldn't bear the thought of turning him out into the wilderness.

"You can stay," North finally said, though he didn't look too happy about it.

"Thank you. Thank you, kindly," Jacob said. "I appreciate it. And I won't be any trouble—well, not any more trouble."

North nodded toward the door. "You can help me with the stock."

"Sure thing." Jacob gathered his shirt and hat and went outside, giving Lily a quick, grateful smile as he went past.

Lily and North faced each other in the quiet cabin. The heat and desire they'd shared only moments ago still simmered, but was abandoned for now.

"Do you think Jacob is telling the truth?" Lily asked, the little knot of fear still humming in her stomach. "Do you think he might really be helping the army with their expedition plans in secret?"

"Jacob isn't involved with the army," North told her without hesitation.

"How can you be so sure?" Lily asked. North knew the men at the fort much better than she did, yet she still couldn't help but wonder—and worry.

"Because I know he isn't," North said.

He said it with a finality intended to end their conversation, but Lily couldn't let it go that easily.

"Then why did the men at the fort suspect him?" she asked.

"Somebody who didn't like Jacob might have made up the story. Somebody might have misinterpreted something he did or said," North told her. "I don't know."

She wished he'd had some concrete explanation, something that might relieve her anxiety.

"Do you think they would have really…killed him?" she asked.

"Yes," North said. "They would have."

Well, that statement certainly hadn't made her feel any better. Lily moved on to the next situation they needed to address.

"What are we going to do with him?" she asked, gesturing toward the door.

"Send him on his way," North said, then added sourly, "The sooner, the better."

Jacob talked nearly nonstop through supper, seemingly content at their table, happy to have someone to visit with after the time he'd spent on the prairie alone. Under other circumstances, Lily would have enjoyed his company, the conversation, his news about activities and people at the fort.

North was quiet—more quiet than usual. He ate, replied when spoken to, but his thoughts seemed elsewhere.

At first Lily thought he was brooding about their near tryst this afternoon that Jacob's presence had interrupted, but wasn't completely convinced that was the problem. She suspected that something else was on North's mind.

Especially after he rose from the table and left the cabin without a word to anybody.

"Let me clean up these dishes for you, Miss Lily," Jacob offered, as he rose from his table, and began gathering plates.

"No, Jacob, that wouldn't be right. I can't let you tackle this job alone," Lily insisted.

"Well, shoot, Miss Lily, after all the cleaning up I did in that kitchen at the fort for so long, these few little ol' dishes here don't amount to hardly nothing," Jacob assured her. "Besides, I owe you all a debt of gratitude, and I intend to pay you back."

"Well, thank you," Lily said, and decided to accept Jacob's generous offer. A night off from doing dishes did sound good.

But without that chore to perform after supper, Lily didn't know how to occupy herself. She considered returning to her journal again to document her visit to the Cheyenne village. She wanted to detail everything—well, almost everything—that had happened there while it was still fresh in her mind.

But, instead, she decided her journal could wait. She'd see to it later. Lily went outside in the closing darkness, breathing in the fresh air. She spotted North standing in the corral amid the herd of horses, talking softly to a bay mare.

He seemed at ease among the animals, she thought as she walked over. She also thought that conversing with horses was preferable to keeping company with a number of people she knew. Tom Carson, for one.

Lily leaned on the top board of the fence and looked over the horses.

"Tom Carson's horses are still here," she noticed. "Has he changed his mind about your deal?"

North gave the mare a final pat on the neck. She wheeled and joined the other horses on the other side of the corral.

He walked over to the fence. "Carson had some things to take care of. He's coming for them tomorrow or the next day."

"I hope he lets Grace come with him," Lily said.

She wanted to talk with Grace again, see if she could find out more about the problems she was having with Tom. Surely, there had to be something she could to do help her new friend.

Another thought occurred to Lily, this one even more alarming.

"What if he sees Jacob?" she asked. "What if when Tom comes over, he sees Jacob?"

After the way Tom talked about the army expedition when he was last here, goodness knows what he might do if he spotted Jacob at the cabin.

"The boy isn't involved with the army. Stop worrying,'' North said, waving away her concern. He headed into the barn.

Lily returned to the cabin, silently willing North's words to sink in, to calm her jitters. She should find comfort in his confidence. He knew Tom Carson much better that she did, knew whether he was truly a threat, or simply a big talker. North knew, too, the gossip and rumors that circulated among the men at the fort. He was there often; he heard what was being said.

Yet Lily found no comfort in North's confident remarks. Something still nagged at her.

Lily tossed and turned on the bunk, unable to sleep. Tired though she was from the full, busy day, she couldn't get comfortable, couldn't relax enough to drift off.

How different this bed was from her chamber at Madame DuBois's school and her room in her father's house. Eiderdown quilts and satin bed linens were a far cry from the buffalo robes that covered her now. And she didn't recall ever being as tired back in Saint Louis as she had been working here at the cabin.

Staring up at the dark ceiling, Lily thought back to her first night in the this cabin, when she'd been worried and scared, unsure of what was to become of her.

All these weeks later, she was no longer worried

or scared, but truthfully, she still didn't know what would become of her.

Lily rolled over, squashing the pillow beneath her head. For so long all she'd dreamed of, thought of, hoped for was to go to Virginia and her aunt's home. Join the life there that she'd been raised for.

Now she wasn't so sure that's what she wanted.

North came to her mind, as he did much of the time. Her body warmed at the memory of the intimacies they'd shared at the lake near the Cheyenne village, and what they'd nearly done when they'd returned to the cabin. If Jacob hadn't already been here... Well, the afternoon would have turned out very differently. So different that now Lily questioned whether she really wanted to return to the East.

How could she go now? Lily thought, flopping onto her back once again. How could she possibly leave this place when—

When what? Lily sighed heavily in the quiet cabin, forcing herself to finish her thought. How could she leave this place when her heart belonged to North?

She thought of him out in the barn, sleeping in one of the stalls. Jacob was out there, too. Otherwise, might she go to him right now?

Perhaps it was just as well that they'd decided to allow Jacob to stay with them until he could figure out what to do with himself, Lily thought. Though by the look she'd seen smoldering in North's eyes lately, she didn't think he would agree.

Determinedly, Lily forced her mind onto other matters. It occurred to her once again that Jacob's stay at the cabin might not be all that harmless. Despite all of North's assurances to the contrary, he could bring trouble down on them.

Lily couldn't shake her fear that the men from the fort might come looking for him. They'd shown themselves to be ruthless in their dealings with her. Why would they be any different where Jacob was concerned?

North seemed so certain that Jacob wasn't involved with passing information along to the army. He hadn't hesitated to say so when she'd asked.

But was he really convinced of that, or was he, perhaps, attempting to keep Lily from worrying?

Nor was North concerned, apparently, that Jacob's presence at the cabin might bring trouble. With so few settlers on the prairie, it wouldn't take very long for the men at the fort to figure out where Jacob had gone, track him down, if they truly wanted to punish him for the things they believed he'd done.

Lily rose from the bunk and walked to the window. The full moon was high overhead, its beams bathing the yard and barn in a pale glow.

What would happen if the men from the fort did come to the cabin? Would North turn Jacob over to the men? Lily's blood boiled at the thought. She had no charitable feelings for any of the men at Bent's Fort.

If the men came for Jacob, what would be offered as proof of Jacob's innocence? North's word alone? Surely the vigilantes wouldn't accept his assertion of innocence as easily as Lily had.

Gazing out the window, she wished it wasn't so late. More than anything, she'd like to go to the barn and talk to North again. Have him close his big, strong arms around her, pull her against his chest and whisper in her ear that everything would be fine. He'd seemed so confident, perhaps that would relieve her worry, at last.

To her surprise, Lily caught a glimpse of North exiting the barn. Her heart tumbled in her chest.

Was he coming to the house? To her?

Then Lily chided herself for having such a wanton thought. More than likely, North was going to the corral to check on the horses, or head around back to the outhouse.

But instead he walked to the edge of the forest.

Lily gasped in the quiet cabin as she saw another man waiting there for him, nearly invisible in the shadows. She dropped to her knees instinctively, not wanting to be seen, and peeked over the windowsill.

Their meeting lasted only a few minutes, but long enough for Lily to study the stranger. Tall, thin, long blond hair trailing to his shoulders.

He was the same man she'd seen at the fort, and again at the cabin her first night here. The man North claimed had been a dream.

The man North had lied about.

A knot gathered in Lily's stomach.

Her first instinct was to charge out of the cabin and confront North, demand to know who, exactly this man was, and an explanation of why North hadn't been truthful when she'd asked him about the man before.

But Lily didn't go outside. There was the possibility that it all meant nothing, she told herself as she went back to the bunk. More than likely the man's presence could be explained easily, and she'd feel foolish for confronting North about it.

After all, why would he lie? What possible reason did he have?

Lily laid down and pulled the buffalo robe over her, repeating these thing over and over in her mind. Yet the knot in her stomach didn't go away. Nor did the familiar fear that North wasn't to be fully trusted.

And if she didn't trust him, how could she stay with him?

Chapter Eighteen

"The true test of good breeding is not whether you can give a formal supper or make a proper introduction, but whether you can mingle comfortably and pleasantly with other people."

Lily's two students stared up from their seats at the kitchen table with rapt attention. Hannah had returned to the cabin this morning, more than willing, thankfully, to get on with her lessons.

To Lily's surprise, Jacob had sat down at the table beside her, seemingly as interested in etiquette instruction as she.

Yet Lily couldn't help but wonder if Jacob's motivation to join them wasn't driven by Hannah herself. She was a beautiful girl, something that hadn't escaped Jacob's notice the moment she entered the cabin. She'd seen that look on his face.

Lily understood how he felt. She was anxious to see North again. But for a very different reason.

"Etiquette in its truer sense," Lily went on, drawing on her many hours of instruction at Madame DuBois's school, "concerns itself with rules which make it more comforting and simpler for us to mingle with one another. These are sensible rules of conduct that prevent misunderstandings, make social occasions smooth and comfortable for all concerned."

"Dang…" Jacob murmured, shaking his head in awe. "Where'd you learn all this stuff from, Miss Lily? Did your mama teach you?"

"Boarding school. Many boarding schools, actually. I attended some of the finest institutes in the East for most of my life," she told him.

"And that's what they taught you?" Jacob asked. "Manners and things like that?"

"Students in the schools learned etiquette, of course, but we were also instructed in the arts, music, dancing, language, things of that nature," Lily explained. "All of the things a young woman absolutely must know to run a home, supervise servants, and take her rightful place in polite society."

"That must have been one heck of a school," Jacob said. "What about reading and writing? Did they teach you that, too?"

"Well, yes. Of course."

"Dang…"

"Can you read and write?" Hannah asked him.

Jacob sat up a little straighter. "Sure can. I had

schooling back home in Tennessee. My mama made sure I went. Not a fancy school like Miss Lily went to. We didn't learn manners or nothing like that. But I can read, real good, too.''

''I can read a little,'' Hannah said. ''My father taught me. He said I should learn.''

''I could listen to you read some, if you'd like. Help you out, if you need it,'' Jacob said, his cheeks growing pink at the offer.

Hannah thought over his offer, then nodded. ''All right,'' she said, and turned back to Lily.

She went on with the lesson she'd planned, the lesson she herself had sat through a number of times; as Madame DuBois had said, a young woman could never know too much about etiquette.

''Today we'll learn about making a proper introduction,'' Lily announced to her students, thankful that they seemed more interested in the subject matter than she'd been during her later years of schooling.

''We'll cover the correct form, special introductions, group introductions, the acknowledgment, and correct and incorrect forms of greetings,'' Lily explained.

''Dang…'' Jacob murmured once more.

Lily continued with the lesson, though her mind wasn't on the topic at hand. Last night's mysterious visitor, and the charges leveled against Jacob at the fort crept into her thoughts.

Her uncomfortable feelings about North wouldn't go away, either.

By midafternoon Lily knew she'd had enough, and her students seemed as if they had endured all that anyone could be expected to take on the subject of introductions, for the time being, anyway. She went outside, leaving Jacob and Hannah on their own.

North was outside the corral. The bay mare hung her big head over the fence nudging his chest, seemingly encouraging him to stroke her neck.

"I think you should go to the fort," Lily said, as she joined them. The idea had just come to her and she saw no reason not to present it.

North looked down at her. "Do we need supplies again? I just got—"

"No, not for supplies," Lily said. "I think you should go there and talk to people, find out what's really going on. Find out if Jacob is the one who's been passing information to the army."

"He's not," North told her, and sounded a little annoyed that she'd asked him again.

Yet his easy dismissal of the subject did not ease Lily's mind.

"I don't understand how can you know that for sure," she said.

North didn't answer. He turned his attention to the mare once more.

"What if Jacob is really involved with this?" Lily

proposed. She flung her hand out. "The men of the fort could be out there somewhere right now, looking for him. What if they are? We could be in danger if they find him here with us."

"We're in no danger." North gave the mare a final pat and headed for the barn, then said over his shoulder, "Stop worrying."

"I can't help but worry," Lily called. "And I don't understand why you're not worried, too. Why you're taking this situation so lightly."

North kept walking, offering no response.

The distrust that had simmered in Lily for days now flared into anger.

"Is it because you have something to hide?" she shouted after him.

North stopped. Slowly he turned to face her. His brows were pulled together, his expression hard. Yet he didn't say anything.

"You *are* hiding something, aren't you," Lily declared and walked to him. The realization hit her hard in the stomach, bringing on a sickening feeling.

"Leave this alone, Lily," North said softly, his voice low and controlled.

But she couldn't.

"I saw you meet with a man near the stable at Bent's Fort. A thin man with long blond hair. Who is he?" Lily pressed her lips together. "And don't tell me you don't remember."

"Macy. John Macy," North told her.

"He was that mysterious man you met in the forest last night, wasn't he? And don't tell me it was a dream again. I saw you with him twice here at the cabin, and once at the fort."

"It was business," North said.

"Horse-trading business, conducted in the dead of night, under the cover of darkness?" she demanded.

"Yes."

"And what about the times you've left the cabin? You claimed you were going to the fort, or to see someone about horses, but now I wonder if that's true. Where are you really going?"

"Stop this, Lily," North said. "You're getting yourself worked up over nothing. You're imagining things that aren't there."

She glared up at him, her anger growing. "Fine. If you won't tell me, I'll go to the fort myself and find out what's going on."

Lily whirled and headed for the barn.

North caught her with two long steps and cupped her elbow, bringing her to a halt. She jerked away.

"I don't want you going to the fort," North said.

"Then tell me the truth," she insisted.

Lily folded her arms across her middle and stared up at him, waiting, silently demanding his answer. North stared right back. Minutes dragged by.

"Well?" she asked.

North huffed irritably, then said, "Leave this

alone, Lily. It's none of your business. Stay out of it—for your own good."

"My own good—" She drew in a quick sharp breath as everything suddenly came clear to her. "It's *you*. You're the one giving information to the army."

North just looked at her, admitting nothing. Yet she saw the tightening of his jaw, the quirk of his brow, and knew she was right.

North was giving information to the army about Western expansion.

How could he do such a thing? How could he put himself in this kind of danger?

Fear suddenly chased away her anger. She'd suspected something was going on from the moment she'd seen North with the mysterious man at the fort, this John Macy. Her suspicion had been right.

But now her thoughts ran wild with worry over what might happen to North if the men at Bent's Fort found out what he was up to. They'd kill him. Kill him and not think twice about it.

"I'm right, aren't I?" Lily asked, silently hoping he'd tell her that she wasn't. Offer some proof to the contrary. But he didn't.

North squared his shoulders. "Yes. John Macy is a scout for the army. I pass information to him."

She thought she'd be relieved to know the truth—finally. But anger took over instead.

"You lied to me," she said, her voice low and hard.

"Yes," he said, not bothering to deny it.

"You lied to me. Almost from the moment we met, you've kept the truth from me. You've been secretive and evasive. You lied to my face."

"It was for your own good," North said.

The anger boiling in her changed again, this time bringing on a new realization and a surge of emotion. Tears sprang to her eyes.

"I can't trust you," she said, the words coming out in a strained whisper.

She'd been wrong to trust her father, wrong to trust the men at the fort, but she'd put her faith in North.

And now he'd shown himself to be no more trustworthy than anyone else.

"You've been secretly working for the government! Passing information along to them!" Lily forced back her tears. "What else have you lied to me about?"

"Nothing," North told her.

She gasped, remembering how she'd given herself—almost all of herself—to him yesterday. Humiliation rolled through her.

"I—I don't really know you at all!" she declared, both angered and frightened by the realization.

"Listen, Lily—"

"No."

"Just hear me out."

"No!"

Lily turned away wanting to run from the sight of him. But to her dismay, Tom and Grace Carson stood a short distance away. Her anger cooled. She felt North grow tense beside her.

How much had Tom Carson overheard?

"Afternoon," Tom called. His tone was cautious, his expression tense. He looked back and forth between the two of them. "I've come to pick up my horses."

Lily spared North a final, quick look, then pushed aside her emotions. She went to Grace, forcing a smile on her face.

"Please, come inside," she said.

Grace glanced up at her husband, but this time she didn't wait for his permission. She hurried away with Lily into the cabin.

Belatedly, Lily wondered where Jacob and Hannah had gone. They weren't in the cabin, she was relieved to see, so they must have gone into the forest somewhere. She said a quick prayer that they would keep out of sight and not return until after the Carsons left.

"Please, sit down," Lily offered, making an effort to compose herself. She drew in a large, calming breath. "Let me make us some coffee. Then we'll sit down and have a nice—"

"I have to talk to you." Grace caught Lily's arm, stilling her.

The pressure of Grace's fingers around her arm startled her. "What is it?"

Grace glanced toward the door, then leaned closer and lowered her voice.

"Tom was at Bent's Fort yesterday," she said, keeping her voice low.

Lily steeled herself, forbidding any emotion to show on her face. If Tom had heard about Jacob, and Grace was about to ask about him, Lily didn't want her expression to give anything away.

"Tom spoke with some people there," Grace went on. "A family. The Millers. We traveled with them from Saint Louis last year on the wagon train when we all came West. They went on to Santa Fe while we stayed here."

"What were they doing at the fort yesterday?" Lily asked, wondering where this bit of news was going.

"They're leaving." Her words came out in a rush of joy and fear. Grace drew in a breath and glanced at the door once more. "Mr. Miller told Tom that they couldn't make a go of it in Santa Fe. His wife didn't like it and neither did their daughters. So they're leaving. Going back East. They were at the fort to buy provisions."

"But why are you—"

"Don't you see? We can leave with them."

"What?"

"You and I. We can put this dreadful place behind us and go back home, where we belong."

Lily just stared at her, unable to speak.

"The Millers are a wonderful family. A kindly
wife and two daughters," Grace explained. "We'll
be safe traveling with them."

"But would they take us in? Would they allow
us to go with them?"

"I'm sure they would," Grace insisted. "Last
year, Mrs. Miller was very concerned about Tom
and me not going on to Santa Fe, about us being
here on the prairie virtually alone. She tried to get
us to come with them, but Tom wouldn't hear of it,
of course."

Lily thought quickly, taking it all in. "How would
we get to the fort?"

Grace drew in a breath. "I've already thought this
through—it's all I've been able to think about since
Tom gave me the news. I'll take one of Tom's
horses and leave just before dawn."

"Tonight?" Lily asked, her thoughts racing.

"We don't dare wait longer," Grace said. "The
Millers have already been at the fort for several
days. They'll head east soon, maybe as early as tomorrow. We must go tonight, or we might miss
them."

"Won't Tom hear you leave?"

"Tom's a sound sleeper. Don't worry, I'll get

away,'' Grace said. "Will you come with me, Lily?''

"I—I don't know.''

"I can bring a horse for you and meet you in the woods, at the stream by that large outcropping of rocks,'' Grace offered. "We can ride to the fort together. It will be safer that way.''

Lily bit her lower lip. "I'm not sure.''

"There are signs of an early winter. Everyone says so. You don't want to be stranded here until spring, do you, Lily?''

"No, of course not, but—''

Grace drew back a little. "Don't tell me you've changed your mind completely and have decided to stay here permanently.''

Lily touched her forehead. "It's not that. It's just that…''

"What?'' Grace asked, searching her face. "What is it, Lily? Why would you stay here when you have the perfect opportunity to leave?''

Lily just looked at her, unable to answer.

"I'll bring a horse for you tonight.'' Grace's expression hardened. "But if you're not there, I'll go without you.''

Chapter Nineteen

Should she leave?

Lily paced back and forth through the cabin, her footsteps sure, even in the darkness. In front of the hearth, Hannah slept soundly, curled up with two buffalo robes, unaware of the weighty issue that plagued Lily and had her walking the floor in the dead of night.

Since Grace Carson had left this afternoon, Lily had done nothing but consider her offer—her escape plan. She'd gone to bed, but slept fitfully, managing only a few hours of sleep, then awakened still troubled, still wrestling with the decision.

Should she go? Or stay?

Lily didn't blame Grace for wanting to leave. Not for a moment. From all appearances, Tom was a dreadful husband. He'd gone back on his promise to her. He'd refused to return to the East. He treated Grace shamefully—probably worse than she let on.

If Grace didn't take this chance to flee, she might never get away from him, or see her home and family again.

No, Lily didn't question Grace's decision.

But what about her own choice?

A choice she'd have to make quickly now, Lily thought, glancing out the window at the waning moon. Dawn was fast approaching.

With a deep sigh, Lily turned and paced toward the bunk in the corner. She'd told North that she'd stay here until Hannah's training was completed. She'd given him her word. It wasn't right of her to walk out on the commitment she'd made.

But after all the lies he'd told, why should she worry about keeping her word?

Another idea intruded on Lily's thoughts, this one even more troubling. After all the other lies North had told, could she trust him to take her to her aunt Maribel's home in Virginia?

The trip was long—months long. It would be difficult and expensive. Had she been foolish to think North would actually deliver her to her aunt's doorstep?

Lily spun around, pacing toward the door. What if tonight was the only opportunity she'd get to leave this place?

Pressing her lips together, Lily turned around, once more pacing in the direction of the bunk. This time she stopped, seeing the rumpled buffalo robes faint in the moonlight.

If things had gone differently yesterday, she'd have lain in the bunk with North. They'd have shared the most intimate act possible between a man and a woman.

Heat rushed through her at the memory. She'd thought she'd fallen in love with him.

But she'd also thought she knew what kind of man North was.

Lily turned away and touched her fingertips to her forehead. Now she wasn't sure of anything.

Except that right now was her best chance—perhaps her only chance—to leave.

Lily dressed quickly, silently, keeping an eye on Hannah. The girl didn't stir, didn't rouse from her sleep.

With a final look around the cabin, Lily gathered what few of her belongings would fit in a sack, and slipped out the door into the night.

Fighting the urge to run, Lily crept silently into the woods near the cabin. At the tree line she stopped, turned back toward the barn, expecting North to charge out and stop her. But all was silent.

Indecision sawed through Lily. For an instant, she wished he would hear her, come outside, spot her among the trees, stop her. Her heart ached suddenly with the wish that he would tell her he was sorry, tell her he'd never lie to her again, that he would always keep his word, no matter what.

But she saw no sign of him. Lily pushed on.

In the sack she'd slung over her shoulder, Lily had placed a few articles of clothing, one of her mother's china plates, her journal and some of her personal items. The weight of the sack was nearly nothing.

Tears pressed against Lily's eyes. She'd come West with high hopes of getting to know her father, starting a business, building a future. Now she was leaving with little more than the clothes on her back. She'd left most everything else behind.

Including her heart?

North sprang to her mind, but she pushed him away, concentrating on the lies he'd told her. The man wasn't trustworthy. How could she build a life under those circumstances?

In the moonlight, Lily made her way through the woods to the spot near the stream and the large outcropping of rocks that Grace had described, expecting to find her waiting with the two horses, as promised. She wasn't there.

A sick feeling crept into Lily's stomach. What if something had happened to Grace? What if Tom had discovered her plan? What if she wasn't coming?

Visions of what Tom might do to Grace if he caught her trying to leave caused her to cringe.

Lily pushed the thoughts away, determined to

think only the best. Grace was fine. She'd come. She would…surely, she would.

Lily had never felt so alone in her life. She hunkered down near the base of a large oak tree, drawing up her knees, trying to make herself as small as possible. Minutes dragged by.

She wished now that she'd asked North take her to the Carsons' cabin at some point over these past weeks. Since she didn't know where it was, all she could do was sit here and wait.

And just how long should she wait? Lily didn't know. Time seemed to creep by.

Finally, she heard a rustling in the darkness. She shrank against the tree trunk, trying to make herself even smaller, her heart beating faster.

Was it North? Had he realized she was gone and come looking for her?

Had Tom seen Grace leave and followed?

Images of army deserters and renegade Indians flew into Lily's mind.

She squinted into the darkness. A horse and rider. Another horse.

Grace.

She looked small and frail atop the big horse, her hands uncomfortable on the reins. Even in the dim light, Lily saw fear in the tight lines of her face.

"I was afraid you weren't coming," Lily said, stepping away from the tree.

"I was afraid *you* weren't," Grace said, handing her the reins of the horse she was leading.

Lily tied her sack of meager belongings onto the saddle, noting that Grace had brought little more than she had; Grace was probably glad to leave everything behind.

"You didn't have any trouble getting away from Tom, did you?"

"He was sleeping when I left," Grace explained. "I left him a note saying I'd gone out to pick berries. He'll find it when he wakes up. That should give us several hours before he realizes I'm not coming back. And when he does, he'll look for me in the woods. He won't think I've gone to the fort."

Lily wondered if perhaps she should have done the same. What would North do when he awoke and realized she wasn't there? Since he'd find none of his horses missing, the last thing he'd suspect was that she was headed toward Bent's Fort.

Yet would he worry, wonder? Search the woods? Fear that something dreadful had happened to her?

"Are you sure about this?" Grace asked, seeming to read her thoughts.

Lily pulled herself into the saddle, the leather creaking as she seated herself. She didn't want to think about North anymore.

"Yes, I'm sure," Lily told her, forcing conviction into her voice. "I'm very sure."

"Then we'd better hurry," Grace said and urged

her horse forward. "If the wagon train leaves the fort today, they'll head out early."

Lily nudged her horse's sides and followed Grace through the trees.

The journey to Bent's Fort wasn't overly long. But neither Grace nor Lily were familiar with the trail, and they had only the moon to light their way.

Twice they stopped, undecided on which way they should proceed. Lily searched her memory, recalling the details of the terrain she'd etched into her mind the day North had taken her from the fort, and pointed the way. By the time the sun rose behind them, the river and cottonwoods came into view, then Bent's Fort.

Outside the fort sat several wagons. It seemed that most of the travelers were up and about already. Campfires burned. The smell of breakfast hung in the air.

Lily breathed a sign of relief: the train hadn't left yet.

She pulled her horse to a stop and signaled Grace to do the same.

"It would be better if you approached the Miller family alone, don't you think?" Lily said. "You're already acquainted with them. They don't know me at all."

Grace nodded. "All right."

"You should stay outside the fort," Lily said. "In case…"

Grace blanched. "In case Tom realizes the horses are gone and comes looking for me."

"I'll take our horses inside the fort," Lily told her. "I know a spot where they won't be easily noticed. In case…"

Grace dismounted, untied the sack containing her belongings and handed the reins to Lily.

"Good luck," Lily said.

Grace drew in a breath, steeling herself, then headed toward the wagon. Lily nudged her horse, and rode into the fort.

She didn't ride through the plaza, but instead turned by the council room and rode past the rear of the building to the alley near the stable. No one was around, thankfully. Though she herself didn't have a reason to hide, she didn't want to advertise her presence at the fort.

Lily tied the two horses to the corral fence.

North leaped into her mind. On this same spot she'd watched from her hiding place among the clutter of crates and boxes, and seen him work some sort of magic on the nervous, unruly stallion. Her heart ached a little at the memory of that day…of him.

Lily pushed North from her mind, again telling herself that she didn't want to think about him anymore.

Another unwelcome thought flashed in her mind: What if the Miller family refused to help?

She had no idea what Grace and she would do if that happened. Lily decided to push that notion from her mind as well. No sense borrowing trouble.

She'd intended to once more sequester herself in the safety of the alley clutter, wait what she hoped would be sufficient time, then return to the wagons out front and see what Grace had arranged.

But instead of hiding, she stepped through the passageway near the carpenter shop and looked into the plaza, keeping herself in the early-morning shadows as best she could.

Her gaze settled immediately on the room where she'd lived with her father, the room where she'd tried to care for him, the room where he'd died.

What would he think of her if he saw her now? After all the money he'd spent sending her to the finest academies for young ladies, he'd surely be shocked.

Yet she wasn't sure he'd be disappointed.

Lily wished she'd thought to bring wildflowers from the woods so she could put them on his grave.

At the early hour, the fort had already come to life. Unkempt men in buckskins, traders, bearded mountain men stood together talking, smoking. The smell of baking bread and roasting meat wound through the air. The blacksmith's hammer clanged.

A little smile came to Lily's lips. How familiar—how welcome—it all seemed. Weeks ago when she'd first come to this place, everything had seemed so strange, so foreign. She'd felt completely out of place. She'd been frightened at simply looking out her window, let alone walking across the plaza.

Now she was tempted to go up to these wild-haired men and strike up a conversation. She wished she could saunter into the kitchen, talk to the cook about spices, and exchange recipes.

What had changed here at the fort that she now felt this way?

A little jolt shook Lily as she realized that nothing here had changed.

She had changed.

Lily turned back into the alley and slipped behind the crates and boxes.

How was she ever going to be happy at Aunt Maribel's now?

Time dragged by with Lily refusing to allow herself to think heavily on the recent circumstances of her life, or the events that lay ahead. Instead, she thought about the delicious smells emanating from the kitchen and listened to her own stomach growl. When she couldn't stand it any longer, she left the alley and headed toward the plaza.

More men were out and about now, a steady stream flowing in and out of the dining room, the trade room. As before, they turned her way, staring, watching. She recognized a few of them, but didn't spot the three men who'd attempted to turn her into a prostitute. Hiram Fredericks and the others were here at the fort somewhere, though, she was sure of it.

A horse and rider galloped through the gate, sending two men scurrying out of the way. Outside the trade room, the rider swung down from the saddle and rushed inside.

Lily's breath caught.

Tom Carson.

Chapter Twenty

Tom Carson. At the fort. Lily's heart thundered in her chest. He'd come here for only one reason.

Her gaze darted out the gate to the wagons that were preparing to depart. Had Tom seen Grace talking to the Millers when he'd ridden past? Yet if he had, why had he gone into the trade room?

Lily made her way across the plaza and out the gate, then hurried from wagon to wagon until she spotted Grace standing with an older woman, whom she believed to be Mrs. Miller. A man—Mr. Miller, surely—was grousing at two young girls who were, apparently, not loading supplies into their wagon to his satisfaction.

"I have to talk to you," Lily whispered to Grace, coming up behind her. She offered a quick apology to Mrs. Miller and pulled Grace around to the far side of the wagon, out of the view of the fort.

"Tom," Lily whispered, breathless. "Tom's here."

"*What?*" Panic sharpened Grace's features. "He can't be."

"He must have awakened right after you left," Lily speculated, "and not believed the note you left him. He must have seen that two of his horses were missing and figured that you had come here."

"This can't be happening. It can't." Grace pressed her lips together, then straightened her shoulders and clenched her fists. "I'm not going back to the cabin with him. I'm not. I don't care what I have to do, I won't go back with him."

"We need to find out what's going on," Lily said, forcing herself to calm down and think. "First, what did the Millers say?"

"They said we could go with them, but—" Grace gulped back a sudden swell of tears. "But if they know Tom's here, and he makes a terrible fuss about me leaving, they might change their minds. They might be too afraid to interfere."

Lily knew she was right. The Millers might not be so sympathetic to Grace's cause with Tom bearing down on them, making threats and insisting she return to the cabin with him.

"Let me find out for sure," Lily said.

"What are you going to do?"

"I saw Tom heading into the trade room. I'll go there and—"

"No!" Grace whispered desperately. "No, you can't let him see you. He'll—"

"He'll do nothing," Lily insisted. "He has no reason to think you and I are together, has he?"

"Well, no…"

"Besides, I'm not going to get any closer to him than I have to. I'll just listen in, try to overhear what's being said."

"All right," Grace said reluctantly.

Lily gestured toward the line of wagons. "When is the train leaving?"

"It will be a while still," Grace said. "Not everyone is packed and ready to go yet."

"Stay out of sight," Lily said. "I'll be back as quickly as I can."

Grace caught her arm. "Be careful."

"I will."

Grace climbed into the wagon as Lily made her way back to the fort.

Surely no other human being had ever garnered so much attention at the fort as Lily had, so she couldn't simply stroll across the plaza, linger outside the trade room and eavesdrop unnoticed. Instead, she ducked behind the building, located what she thought was the trade room's window, pulled over a wooden keg and climbed up.

Peeking into the room, she saw a crowd of a dozen or so men gathered around Tom Carson. His audience was intent on what he was saying, luckily, so she wouldn't likely be noticed at the window.

Lily recognized many of the faces in the crowd. Hiram Fredericks, Oliver Sykes she knew by name. Others looked familiar.

"I'm telling you I saw him," Tom Carson was saying. His voice was loud, his tone angry. "Saw him with my own two eyes. Last night."

Hiram Fredericks stroked his chin thoughtfully. "I still can't believe that boy would do something like this. I just didn't think Jacob had it in him."

Stunned, Lily realized it wasn't his wife Tom was discussing, but Jacob Tanner and his supposed connection to the army expedition.

Dread knotted Lily's stomach. As she feared, Tom must have seen Jacob near the cabin last night, and now he'd come here this morning to report his sighting and cause more trouble.

That worthless, miserable excuse for a husband. Lily almost wanted to shout at him. His own wife was leaving him—planning her escape scarcely yards away—and he didn't even know it.

"Did you catch the boy?" Sykes asked.

"I didn't want to tip my hand, let on that I'd seen him. Not with just me by myself. Didn't want him to get scared and run off again." Carson narrowed his eyes. "But I know exactly where to find him."

"Who'd a thought it?" Fredericks mused, still

mulling over his surprise at Jacob's believed betrayal.

"Here's the thing," Carson said, leaning closer to the men. "I heard some talk last night, too. That Tanner boy didn't do this all by himself. He had help."

A hush fell over the trade room. The men inched a little closer to Carson.

Lily drew in a quick breath.

"From who?" Sykes asked at last.

Carson waited another moment while the drama built. Finally he said, "From the man whose cabin I spotted him near last night."

He let another few seconds pass. "North Walker."

A murmur went through the crowd of men.

Lily felt dizzy.

"Damn…" Fredericks shook his head, then took a big, resigned breath. "Well, I guess that makes sense."

Heads nodded in agreement.

"Walker's here at the fort real often, always talking to traders and trappers who've been West," Fredericks said. "I've seen him with that Macy fellow right often, too, the one that scouts for the army sometimes."

"And don't forget," Sykes said ominously, "Walker is half-Indian."

Another rumble went through the gathering. Heads bobbed.

"I say we take care of this right now," Carson declared, with an ugly enthusiasm in his voice. "I say we head out to Walker's cabin this morning, and get things…handled."

Fredericks and Sykes looked at each other for a long moment.

Lily said a silent prayer that the men wouldn't let Tom Carson goad them into retaliating against North. Surely one of them would have sense enough to see what they were doing wasn't right.

But her prayers weren't to be answered.

"Help yourselves to ammo," Fredericks said, waving the men toward the shelves behind him. "Let's get this over and done with quick as we can."

Lily ducked down from the window, dread knotting her stomach. The men were going after North.

And when they found him, they would kill him.

She leaped from the wooden keg and raced to the alley. Thankfully, the horses she'd left there earlier were still tied to the fence. She climbed into the saddle, took the back way behind the building, and rode out to the Miller's wagon.

"I have to go," Lily said, drawing up alongside the tailgate.

Grace hung back in the shadows. "Go? You can't go. We're leaving soon."

The horse tossed its head, picking up Lily's anxiety. She struggled to keep it under control.

"I'll catch up with the train this afternoon," Lily said. "And don't worry. Tom doesn't know you're here. You're safe."

"But, Lily—"

"I have to go." She kicked her horse and headed away from the fort.

The mare North had sold to Tom Carson, and Grace had given her this morning, was young and strong. She covered the ground quickly.

Lily's thoughts raced along with the horse's pounding hoofs. She had to get to North. She had to warn him. The men were coming after him— probably only a few minutes behind her. If she didn't get there quickly, find him, tell him they were coming, the men would kill him.

When she reached the woods, Lily pulled the horse back as they made their way through the trees. Finally, the cabin came into sight.

"North!" she called, pushing the mare to a gallop again.

She rode to the barn and shouted his name once more, then wheeled the mare around and rode to the cabin.

"North!"

The door opened and Jacob came outside, wide-eyed and smiling.

"Good gracious, Miss Lily, where the heck have

you been this morning?'' he asked, ambling over to the hitching rail.

Lily swung down from the horse and thrust the reins at Jacob.

''Where's North?'' she demanded.

''We've been looking all over for you,'' Jacob said. ''Where'd you run off to?''

''Jacob!'' Lily shouted, fighting to hold her temper in check. ''Where's North?''

Jacob looked startled and slightly offended. ''He took off out of here looking for you. Hannah's looking, too. She headed toward the Cheyenne village, thinking maybe you went up there.''

Lily's heart sank. North and Hannah were both gone? Somehow, she had to find them. All of them had to leave immediately. None of them was safe here at the cabin—not for long, anyway.

''Jacob, where did North go, exactly?'' Lily asked. ''Do you know?''

He thought for a moment, twisting his lips and scrunching his brows together.

''Well, no, not exactly,'' Jacob said.

''Which direction did he take?'' she asked, her gaze sweeping the area.

''I didn't rightly notice,'' Jacob told her. ''He said for me to stay here at the cabin 'cause I don't hardly know my way around through these woods, and he didn't want me getting lost on top of everything else.''

"I'll have to find him, somehow."

"If you came back, he told me I was to fire his rifle in the air."

"What?" Lily nearly leaped at him. "Then go fire the rifle! And hurry!"

"Well...all right," Jacob said, drawing back from her slightly.

"This is a matter of life and death!" she exclaimed, exasperated.

Jacob retrieved the rifle from the cabin and fired a shot into the air. The sound cracked, echoing through the still forest, driving a covey of birds from the high treetops.

"Come inside, Jacob."

Lily untied her sack from the saddle and latched onto his arm, pulling him into the cabin with her. She pointed toward the stove.

"Get some food together, as much as you can carry. Make two sacks. And fill the canteens."

"What's going on, Miss Lily?" he asked, standing there frowning at her.

"There's a party of vigilantes coming from the fort. They're after you and North."

He gasped. "Me and—"

"We have to leave here—all of us."

Jacob's eyes widened. "Oh, my Lord..."

"Get to work," Lily told him. "And hurry. We haven't much time."

While Jacob got the food together and filled two

canteens, Lily sat down at the table, pulled her journal from her sack, flipped to the back page and started writing furiously.

"If'n you don't mind me saying so, Miss Lily, this don't hardly seem like the time to be recording your personal thoughts."

"I'm writing a—"

Hoofs pounded the ground outside. Lily jumped up and raced to the window.

North.

Emotion surged through her. She tore outside.

He swung down from the stallion before it had completely stopped, his face tight with anger. He crossed to Lily in two long strides and grasped her shoulders.

"What the hell do you think you're doing running off! I didn't know where you were. I've been looking all over for you—"

"We have to leave!" Lily exclaimed.

"—thinking that you'd been hurt, or were lost! Where the hell have you—"

"We have to leave!" Lily told him again, shaking off his hands. "The men at the fort, they know. They know about Jacob being here. They know about you, North. They know what you've been doing."

North froze, watching her, listening.

"They're on their way here to get you and Jacob,'' Lily said. ''They're no more than a half hour behind me, maybe less.''

He turned toward the woods and the trail that led to the fort. Lily saw him mind working, sure she knew what he was thinking.

''We can't fight them,'' she said, catching hold of his arm. ''There's a dozen of them, at least. We have to go.''

North pulled away from her, cursed, paced back and forth for a moment. Then he turned to her.

''I'll get two fresh horses. Jacob and I will ride into the hills. You and Hannah go to the Cheyenne village. I'll come back as soon as it's safe.''

''It will never be safe,'' she insisted. ''Don't you see? We'll never be safe here at the cabin again.''

North paused, her words sinking in. ''I have a plan,'' Lily said. ''There's a wagon train leaving the fort this morning headed back East. We'll send—''

''A wagon train?'' North frowned. ''How do you know about a wagon train?''

She didn't answer, just pushed on. ''Grace is on the train. We'll—''

''Grace?''

''We'll send Hannah and Jacob there. They can catch up easily. I'll write a letter of introduction to my aunt Maribel and they can stay with her until things are sorted out.''

''Your aunt? In Virginia?''

''You wanted Hannah to go there,'' Lily said.

"Jacob can watch out for her until they arrive. He has family in Tennessee."

North's expression hardened, then he nodded. "Hannah and Jacob should go. You should go—"

"No. The Millers won't let all of us travel with them. They won't have room. But they will take Grace and one other person—"

"How do you know—"

"—and Mr. Miller will be anxious for Jacob's help, so they'll take him, too." Lily pushed her chin up. "I'm going with you."

"The hell you will."

"I'm going."

North shook his head. "You'll only slow me down."

"No, I won't."

"Look, Lily, it's too dangerous. You can't—"

"I'm going with you!"

They looked at each other for a long, hard moment. Lily wouldn't give in, and she wouldn't back away. Not now. Not after what she'd been through.

She waved toward the trail to the fort. "We don't have time to argue over this. I'm going with you and that's final."

"All right, then," North finally said. "Let's go."

Chapter Twenty-One

Hannah, too, heard the rifle shot and returned to the cabin a few minutes later. Lily didn't give her any time to ask questions, just explained to her what had happened at the fort. Hannah jumped in helping Jacob pack what they could carry.

"You should wear one of my dresses," Lily said from the table, gesturing to the trunk in the corner. "And take another one with you."

Hannah and Jacob both looked at her, each thinking the same thing but not saying it aloud: if Hannah appeared at the wagon train in her doeskin dress and moccasins, the travelers might turn her away. In Eastern garb, she looked like a white woman.

"Here, Jacob," Lily said, rising from the table. She passed him her journal. "When you get to Saint Louis, take this to the newspaper. I wrote the address and name of the man you're to see. He'll pay you for my journal, so you'll have traveling money.''

"Yes, ma'am,'' Jacob said, shoving it into one of the sacks.

"My aunt's name and address is in there, too. I've written her a letter, explaining things, asking her to take in Hannah. You, too, if you want,'' Lily said, hoping her hastily scribbled letter made sense. "Now you'd better go help North with the horses.''

Lily stole glances out the window as she assisted Hannah into one of her dresses, closing fasteners, tying ribbons. Her ears strained for the sound of approaching horses.

"There. All done,'' she said, stepping back and looking Hannah up and down with a critical eye. In this dress, and with her blond hair, the girl would never be thought of as Indian.

"You look very Eastern,'' Lily said.

Hannah ran her hands down the skirt of the dress, obviously a little uncomfortable in the gown. "I don't know if I can manage.''

"You'll do fine,'' Lily told her, sure that she would.

She drew in a breath and took one last look around the cabin. "We'd better go.''

North waited outside with three horses. He had more riding horses, but only three saddles. He'd already tied the food sack and canteen that Jacob had prepared to the saddles of two of the horses.

"You can catch up with the wagon train easily. Hannah knows the way," North said to Jacob. "If something happens and you miss it, or they won't take you in, go to the Cheyenne village."

"Yes, sir," Jacob said.

The two men shook hands. Lily rushed forward and gave Jacob a solid hug. "You two be careful. Watch out for each other. And tell my aunt I love her when you get to Virginia."

"Yes, Miss Lily, I will," Jacob assured her, then climbed into the saddle.

Lily gave Hannah a hug, then held her at arm's length. "Aunt Maribel will take care of everything once you get to her house. She's a very kind woman. You'll like her. She'll like you, too."

Hannah nodded quickly, as if wanting to believe what Lily had said, but still was unsure.

North stepped forward. He and Hannah looked at each other, neither moving, yet Lily saw the distress in both their gazes.

It had been North's plan all along for Hannah to leave. She'd agreed to go. But now that the time had arrived—and so much more quickly than any of them had imagined—parting was difficult.

Both knew that they would not likely see each other again. Ever.

North caught her in a bear hug and pulled her against him. Hannah hung in his embrace, stretching up on her toes to touch her cheek against his. Then he set her away.

"You'd better go," he said to Jacob.

The younger man climbed into the saddle. North caught Hannah's foot and hoisted her up behind him.

Lily stood beside the horse, a hundred thoughts racing through her mind. She knew very well that she may never see either of them again.

She wanted to caution them about what lay waiting on the trip, at her aunt's, in the world. But instead she simply squeezed both their hands a final time, and watched them ride away.

She turned to North. Their gazes met. The desperation of the situation showed on both their faces.

North grabbed her waist, pulling her hard against him. Lily flung her arms around his neck. Their mouths met in a wet, hot kiss that seared them both together.

North pulled away. "Go to the village."

Lily just looked at him, sure that she hadn't heard him correctly. "No..."

"You'll be safe there."

"But you—"

"I'm going to ride toward the fort and find these men," he told her.

Lily twisted her fists into the front of his shirt. "No!"

"I have to be sure they'll follow me, and not go

after Jacob and Hannah.'' North grasped her shoulders. ''Don't you see, Lily, it's the only way we can know for certain they'll be safe.''

No. No, she didn't want him to do it. She didn't want him to go at all—certainly not without her. But he was right.

''Promise me,'' she whispered. ''Promise me you'll be careful.''

He pulled her hands from the front of his shirt. ''I'll meet you at the village as soon as I can.''

North helped her into the saddle, then mounted his horse. He waited.

Lily's heart ached. Her stomach knotted, knowing full well this may be the last time she saw him.

Then she turned her horse and trotted to the tree line. She stopped and looked back. North waved, then galloped away.

Lily headed toward the village, letting the horse pick its own path through the trees. Her head told her it was the right thing to do. But her heart said something entirely different.

In her mind, Lily's future stretched out before her. What if something happened to North? What if the men at the fort found him?

What if she absolutely never saw him again?

Lily pulled the horse to a stop. She couldn't leave it at that.

She rose in the stirrups, getting her bearings. Jacob and Hannah had headed south to intercept the

wagon train. North had ridden toward the fort,
searching for the men who were bent on tracking
him down. He didn't intend to confront them, just
lead them away from Jacob and Hannah and the
Cheyenne village. That meant he'd ride north.

Lily drew in a breath and headed in that direction.

She'd guessed right.

From her vantage point, Lily caught sight of
North. Her heart rate picked up. Nearly a dozen men
followed him.

North rode hard. Each moment that passed, each
stride of his horse, took the vigilantes farther and
farther away from Jacob and Hannah, just as North
had wanted.

The leather reins slipped through Lily's sweaty
palms. She gathered them back in. Now, this moment, was her last chance to change her mind.

She didn't.

Lily touched her heels to the horse's sides and the
mare leaped forward.

She bit down on her lip as she pushed the mare
through the trees. Her heart pounded. The horse
raced down a ravine, jumped a fallen tree, then
broke from the forest slightly ahead of North.

Lily crouched low in the saddle, urging the horse
on. The mare was no match for North's bigger,
stronger stallion. She'd have to push her hard to
keep up.

Hooves pounded the earth behind her, drawing nearer, until she saw North pull alongside. Fury shone in his eyes. Lily chanced a glance over her shoulder. The band of vigilantes wasn't far behind.

Lily nudged the mare again, bringing her close to the stallion, letting North take the lead. He knew the lay of the land better than she, and probably better than the men who followed.

Gradually, they turned west and into the trees again. The terrain caused them to slow. Lily looked over her shoulder once more, hoping the men would abandon the chase. They didn't.

Deeper they rode into the forest. Up and down hills, leaves and plants rustling under the punishing hooves of the horses. North jumped a stream. Cold water splashed up on Lily as she followed. Her mare stumbled, but recovered and continued on. She trailed North up a steep slope and around an outcropping of rocks. He pulled back on the reins and his horse bounded to a stop.

"Get down," he shouted, as he swung out of the saddle.

Lily drew back on the reins. Her mare tossed its head and danced in a tight circle. As they swung around, her gaze swept the forest behind them. She couldn't see the men, but she knew they hadn't given up, hadn't stopped.

North didn't explain, or wait for her. He grasped

her waist and pulled her from the saddle. Lily's knees buckled. She caught his arm to stand upright.

"What are you doing?" she asked, breathing heavily.

A shot rang out. North pushed her down on the forest floor behind the rocks, then slapped both horses on the rump. They lurched forward and disappeared up the slope and into the trees. North dropped to the ground beside Lily.

Lying on his belly, his face inches from hers, North's eyes narrowed with raw fury.

"What the hell do you think you're doing?" he shouted. "I told you to go to the village. Why did you come here? I told you what to do. I told you where I wanted you to go. I told you—"

"*Now* you want to talk?" she demanded and rolled her eyes.

He glared at her.

She gestured toward the woods on the other side of the rocks. "They're shooting at us."

North pushed her down again and got to his knees. He peered around the rock. Another shot pierced the air, this one digging into the dirt a yard away.

Lily scrambled closer to the rock. "What are we going to do?"

"Escape," North said, raising up once more to see the men.

Lily's eyes widened. "Then why did we stop? Why did you drive the horses off? Why—"

"Listen."

She cringed as another bullet cut through the still forest, this one striking the rock above her head, then ricocheting through the trees.

"All I hear is those men trying to kill us," Lily told him.

"Shh." North touched his fingers to his lips. "Listen closely."

Lily closed her eyes, tuning out the shots that echoed through the trees, the pounding of her own heart.

Water. Rushing water.

Her eyes popped open.

"A waterfall," she said. "Nearby."

"The falls empty into a river just a few yards away." North rose from a crouch to spy on the vigilantes again. He ducked quickly as more shots rang out. He glanced at Lily. "That's where we're going."

"To the river?" Lily exclaimed. Her mind whirled. "Is there a boat? A canoe? How will we—"

North pointed through the trees. "Go that way. You'll see the river."

"But what will you—"

"I'll be right behind you." He glanced over the rocks once more. "They're coming. Go!"

Lily crouched low and dashed through the woods, weaving between the trees. She heard shouts behind her. The sound of the rushing water grew louder, stronger. She ran faster then—

With a gasp, she grabbed a tree branch and dug in her heels, wavering for a few seconds at the edge of a cliff. A waterfall plunged into a canyon, breaking over rocks, boiling and churning before it pooled into a river and swept downstream.

North grabbed her arm, startling her once again.

"Let's go!" he shouted, pulling her forward.

"Are you crazy?" Lily jerked her arm away.

North glanced back through the woods. "We have to jump. Now."

Lily heard shouts from the men, and the rustle of leaves on the forest floor as they ran toward them.

"It's our only chance," North told her.

She shook her head frantically. "No—"

"Don't be afraid. We'll be all right."

"I—I can't!"

He grasped her chin and turned her face up to his, looking deeply into her eyes. "Don't you trust me, Lily?"

She gasped and pulled back from him. *No!* her mind screamed. No, she didn't trust him. He'd deceived her, lied to her, kept secrets from her—and now he wanted her to *jump off a cliff* with him?

North looked back at the men. "Lily, let's go!"

She glanced behind her. The men had fanned out

through the trees, approaching slowly now that they were cornered, pointing rifles at them.

Lily looked down at the rushing water, looked at the men, then up at North. "I—I—"

"You're going to have to trust me, Lily—whether you want to or not."

North locked his arm around her waist, grabbed her arm and rushed toward the edge of the cliff. Lily screamed.

They jumped.

Chapter Twenty-Two

"Oh…" Lily moaned as she fell onto the soft, damp earth. Spray from the waterfall covered her with a fine mist.

"Shh."

She felt North's arms beneath her, lifting her. The world tilted slightly as he carried her backward. Then they both collapsed.

"Shh," he said again, pulling her against him, settling his hand over her mouth.

Another stunned moment passed before Lily realized their leap from the cliff had landed them on a hidden ledge, about halfway down to the river. Now, scooted back against the rocks, an overhang hid them from the view of the vigilantes above.

She drew herself up smaller, closer to North. He gathered her in his arms and held her tight.

Overhead, she heard the men shouting, then talking. Their words were faint above the noise of the roaring waterfall, but she could hear enough to know the vigilantes thought she and North had jumped into the river.

They thought she and North were dead.

She gazed up at North. He'd lived in these woods all his life, knew about this waterfall. But what about the hidden ledge?

After a while, the talking stopped, the men apparently heading back to the fort. Yet North held her against him, refusing to leave the safety of their hiding spot until he was certain the men had given up on them. Minutes dragged by with no voices from above.

Finally, North crept out onto the ledge and looked up at the cliff. He rose to his feet, and waved Lily out with him.

She stood, her legs aching, her body sore from the hard landing. Like North, she gazed up at the cliff and saw no one.

"Please tell me you knew this ledge was here all along," she said.

The smallest hint of a playful grin tugged at his mouth.

"North!"

"Yes," he said quickly. "Yes, I knew the ledge was here."

She looked upward again. The top of the cliff was too high to reach, the walls around them too sheer to climb.

"Now what?" Lily asked.

He turned his gaze toward the river below. Lily looked down, as well.

The water was a good distance below them, churning and rushing away from the falls.

She turned to North. "You think we should jump?"

He didn't answer. He didn't have to. It was their only way out and Lily knew it.

What choice did they have?

Lily shrugged. "Last one in has to make supper tonight."

North grasped her hand, and they jumped together.

"It isn't much farther," North said, shortening his strides to match hers as they hiked uphill through the forest.

Lily held in her sigh of relief, not wanting to expend any unnecessary energy. She had little to spare.

After they'd jumped into the river, they'd floated downstream on the current for several miles before finding a place to climb out. Soaked, tired and weary, Lily had wanted to collapse on the bank and fall sleep, but North hadn't let her. Instead, he'd gotten her up and moving.

They'd been walking through the woods for hours now. The heat of the sun had dried her dress and petticoats, but they were stiff and filthy with mud and dirt. Her hair had come lose from its pins and hung loose down her back. Her shoes squished when she walked.

North was in no better shape. He didn't complain so she didn't, either.

In fact, neither of them spoke at all. What could they say?

To all the world they were dead, their drowning death in the river witnessed by a dozen men from Bent's Fort. The good part of which was that no one else would come looking for North.

The bad part was that they could never go home again.

The cabin, the barn, the outbuilding, everything North had built with his own hands. The horses he'd trained. The supplies he'd traded for. Lily's fixtures, her clothing, her mother's china service. All abandoned. All destined to be looted by the men from the fort, more than likely.

Lily pushed her chin up, telling herself once more that it was enough that they were alive. Nothing else really mattered. But still…

They pressed on through the forest until the trees and underbrush took on a familiar feel. Lily realized where they were and her heart soared.

North knelt behind a stand of trees and pulled Lily down with him.

"The cabin," she said, keeping her voice low. North nodded and she said, "But the men from the fort might be there. They could see us. If they realize we're really not dead—''

''It's possible,'' North said thoughtfully. ''But I think it's more likely that the men will keep looking for Jacob. They think we're dead. They'll be in no rush to ransack the cabin and take what they want.''

A flicker of hope rose in Lily. His idea made sense.

''We'll have to work fast,'' North said. ''Take only what's important.''

Lily paused. ''But what will happen when the men finally do come to the cabin and see that most everything is already gone?''

''They'll figure someone else came across it before they did.'' North grinned. ''We're dead, remember?''

''They got your two horses up by the waterfall,'' Lily said. ''That should satisfy them.''

North left her behind the trees and scouted ahead. After he'd made sure no one was at the cabin, he waved her over.

North went to the barn. Lily dashed inside the cabin, finding a new energy.

North had told her to bring only what was important. But to Lily, everything was important. How would she decide what to bring, and what to leave behind?

She'd take it all.

Frantically, Lily packed her clothing, North's

clothing, buffalo robes, pots, pans, her mother's china service, linens, food supplies, crockery into anything that was available, and carried them outside. North drove the covered wagon over, a string of horses tied off to the back, and they loaded everything inside.

Drawing on the last of her strength, Lily pulled herself up onto the seat. Even with North's help, it was a chore. Her bones ached from fatigue.

North settled onto the seat beside her and picked up the reins. But he hesitated a moment, gazing at the cabin, the barn and outbuildings.

Lily's heart went out to him. He'd built it all. And now he had to leave it. Never to return.

She touched his arm, remembering something he'd told her shortly after she'd arrived at the cabin. "A wise man once told me that a home isn't a roof over your head, but a place in your heart."

North's features softened. "A wise man, huh?"

She grinned. "Well, pretty wise."

North chuckled, then flicked the reins and the wagon lurched forward.

"Where are we going?" Lily asked a few minutes later.

"The Cheyenne village for tonight," North said. "The men from the fort won't go there."

Lily knew that was true. Even if they weren't afraid of entering the village uninvited, they wouldn't ride in demanding North be turned over to them and possibly provoke an incident that might lead to an uprising.

"And tomorrow?" she asked.

"Tomorrow," North said, "I'll take you to your aunt in Virginia."

They reached the village just before nightfall. Exhausted, Lily had struggled to stay awake during the trip. Twice, she'd let her head fall against North's shoulder and had dozed off. Twice, the swaying wagon had jarred her awake.

The men and women of the tribe gathered around the wagon, talking, asking questions, but Lily understood little of what was being said.

"Buffalo scouts watched the wagon train pass by this afternoon, heading east," North told her.

She came more awake now. "Did they see—"

"Yes," North said. "They saw Hannah. At first they feared she'd been kidnapped—"

Lily drew in a sharp breath. "They didn't attack the train, did they?"

"She signaled them that she was all right," North told her.

"What about Jacob? Any sign of him?"

While she'd been sure the Miller family would take Hannah in Lily's place, she wasn't so certain they'd be willing to accept Jacob. But he could sleep outside under the wagon and help Mr. Miller with chores. Surely, they would see how valuable he could be on the trip.

"The scouts don't know Jacob, they couldn't recognize him," North said. "But they saw two men seated up top. One young. One old."

Lily heaved a sigh of relief. "That had to have been Jacob. Mr. Miller was the only man traveling on their wagon."

North just nodded, apparently relieved that Hannah and Jacob had, in fact, gotten away.

Lily touched his arm, another alarming thought penetrating her sleepy brain.

"Do you think the vigilantes will follow the wagon train? Look for Jacob there?"

"I doubt it," North said. "I don't think their anger at him is enough to follow the train."

"You're probably right," Lily said.

Her worry dispelled, fatigue once more sapped her strength. Too tired to go on, Lily gladly went with one of the women who led her to the tepee she'd slept in during her last visit. Lily went inside and immediately fell into a sound sleep.

Hours later, she awoke. Around her the other women still slept. She could hear their steady, even breathing.

Lily's body ached slightly from the difficult day, but sleep had helped. Mostly she was uncomfortable in her filthy dress.

She crept outside into the darkness and followed

the familiar path she'd taken with North on her earlier visit to the village. It wound through the trees to the lake he'd shown her.

Moonlight danced across the still waters. The lake seemed to call to Lily—a call she answered eagerly.

She kicked off her shoes and stockings, then shimmied out of her dress and petticoats anxious to fling herself into the water.

A noise startled her. She whirled and saw a shadow among the trees. Yet standing there in her chemise and pantalettes, she didn't feel the panic to cover herself. Not after what she'd been through today.

North stepped from the trees, his gaze homing in on her as he walked over. She wasn't surprised to see him. Lily's heart stumbled in her chest.

She touched her tangled hair and dipped her gaze. "I'm a mess."

"You're beautiful."

She smiled and felt her cheeks flush. "I was going to bathe in the lake."

"Could we talk first?" North asked.

He wanted to talk? That was certainly odd.

But Lily couldn't deny him. She sat down on the skirt of her dress spread out on the ground. North dropped beside her, close, but not so near that they touched. Still, she felt heat roll off him.

A long moment passed while North gazed across the lake in silence. Lily began to wonder if he'd changed his mind about wanting to talk to her. Then he spoke.

"How did you know about the wagon train leaving the fort this morning?" he asked.

This morning? Was it only this morning? It seemed to Lily that an eternity had passed since she'd met Grace in the woods, then gone on to Bent's Fort.

"Grace told me. She heard the news from Tom. He'd been to the fort," Lily said.

North turned his gaze on her. "Did she tell her husband that she was leaving him?"

She heard a note of suspected betrayal in his voice.

"No," Lily said softly. "She didn't tell Tom. She was afraid of him."

North looked away, allowing several more silent moments to pass, then turned to her again.

"Are you afraid of me, Lily?"

"No," she said quickly. "Of course not."

"Then why did you leave without telling me?" He sounded confused...hurt. "That's what you were doing, wasn't it? Leaving with Grace. Going back East."

"Yes," she admitted and shifted uncomfortably. "I was mad at you. You'd lied to me, kept things from me. I didn't trust you."

"I kept things from you for your own good."

"A lie is still a lie," she told him.

He didn't disagree.

North let a few more minutes pass, then asked, "Why did you come back from the fort and warn me? You could have left, but you didn't."

"Because I love you." The words rolled off Lily's lips easily, quickly, with no hesitation.

North looked hard at her. For a moment, she thought he would kiss her, but he didn't.

"You can go ahead with your bath now," he said, gesturing toward the lake and making no move to rise and give her any privacy.

She touched the drawstring at the top of her chemise. "I wasn't going to wear my underthings."

"Then by all means, go ahead with your bath."

There was a warmth in his voice she'd never heard before. It washed through her, gave her strength…made her reckless with desire.

Lily rose and sauntered to the bank of the lake. With her back to North, she pulled her chemise over her head, dropped her pantalettes and dived into the lake.

The water was cool and silky against her skin as she swam with long languid strokes toward the center of the lake. A splash sounded behind her. She rolled onto her back and saw North swimming toward her, his clothing piled on the shore with hers.

Lily squealed playfully and tried to swim away, but he caught her ankle and pulled her to him. She giggled and he chuckled as they struggled. She planted her hands on his bare shoulders intending to push him under, but instead, his arms circled her and pulled her against him.

Suddenly, nothing was funny anymore.

His chest was warm despite the chilly water as her breasts melted against him. Beneath the water, their thighs brushed. North slid his hand behind her head and covered her mouth with his.

He blended their lips together with exquisite gentleness. Lily leaned her head back, accepting his kiss.

The water around them seemed to grow warmer as North deepened their kiss. Heat arced from him, urging her to want more.

Lily pulled away. North looked surprised, but didn't say anything, didn't protest. Then she swam toward the shore. He followed.

North vaulted up the lake bank first and caught her hand, pulling her out of the water and onto the shore.

In the moonlight, they gazed at each other, the beams dancing off the droplets clinging to their bare skin.

North swept her into his arms and carried her to their pile of clothing a short distance away. He dropped to his knees and laid her there, then stretched out beside her.

North pushed himself up on one elbow and kissed her.

Lily moaned softly as he pressed his fingers into the thickness of her hair. She tipped her head back, welcoming his kiss, twining intimately with him.

His touch was gentle as he drew his hand across her belly, then upward to cup her breast. Then he kissed her there, his mouth creating hot sensations against her cool skin.

She looped her arms around his neck and pressed closer, a need rising in her as she drew her hand across his chest. North groaned and covered her mouth once more with a demanding kiss.

Urgency claimed them both as North moved his hand down the curve of her hip and drew her closer. Lily slid her leg the length of his, touching him intimately.

He kissed her body, tasting her thighs, her hips. Lily writhed at the pleasure of these newfound sensations. Yet she knew they weren't enough.

North looked up at Lily, her head thrown back, her mouth wet with his kisses. She was vulnerable, trusting, ready to give herself to him. His heart swelled with love.

Desire coiled deep within him. North rose above her and she parted her thighs for him. He eased himself into her with the utmost care. For a moment, he nearly lost all control. North gritted his teeth and held back.

Slowly, gently, he moved within her, until she responded with the same desire that claimed him.

Lily threw her arms around his neck and grabbed his hair. All thought vanished from her mind. She moved with him, arching up to him, until great waves of passion broke through her.

North held back longer, until he was certain, then thrust deep inside her, again and again.

"I don't want to take you to your aunt's house in Virginia."

"I don't want to go to my aunt's house in Virginia."

North pushed himself up on his elbow above Lily, his gaze dark and intense in the moonlight.

"You don't?" he asked.

"No, I don't. I want to stay here with you."

"You don't trust me."

Lily touched her finger to his face and stroked his jaw. They'd made love another time, then slept, waking still tangled in each other's arms.

"Building trust is something we'll have to work on," Lily agreed, then smiled. "But I'm willing to give you another chance."

He mulled that over for a moment. "And you won't leave me again?"

"Not as long as you don't lie to me again."

"Fair enough," North said. "Does that mean you'll marry me?"

"Are you asking me to marry you?"

"Yes."

"Do you love me?"

"Ah, Lily…" North took her hand snugly in his and kissed it gently. "I love you with all my heart. Please marry me."

Lily gulped, emotion rising in her. "I love you, North. I'll marry you."

He kissed her softly, sealing their decision.

"Where will we live?" Lily asked.

"Up north," he said. "We'll find a place there and start over."

"But what about your work with the government? Your work with the Indians?" Lily asked. She couldn't imagine him abandoning his people. "I know how strongly you feel about helping your tribe. You can't just walk away from everything."

"I don't intend to," North said. "There is much to be done and I will find a way to do it—just not anywhere near Bent's Fort."

Lily sighed contentedly and snuggled closer, resting her head against his chest. She felt his body relax against hers in much the same way.

"We'll have quite a story to tell our grandchildren," Lily said. "Especially about our leap off the cliff today, and our jump into the river."

"Grandchildren..." North smiled and snuggled closer to Lily, tucking her head beneath his chin and looping his arms around her. "Children... grandchildren...yes, we'll have lots of both."

After a few moments, he heard Lily's gentle, even breathing. He closed his eyes and fell asleep, content with her beside him.

Epilogue

North came awake slowly, his body warm with the afterglow of lovemaking and a contentedness he'd never experienced before. The gray of dawn had settled over the valley. A mist rose from the lake.

Beside him, Lily slept peacefully, her bare body curled intimately against him. He sighed, never wanting to move from this spot.

Yet something troubled him. Something unseen, unknown. Gently, North eased Lily from his shoulder and sat up. His gaze swept the trees, the banks of the lake, but he saw no one.

The strange feeling grew stronger. In the mist rising from the lake he sensed something. A figure. Himself? In the future? He sensed trouble and a plea for help.

"Trust what you sense, not what you see," he murmured.

A warmth settled in his chest, snug around his

heart, bringing with it a newfound sense of well-being.

Lily's eyes fluttered open. She smiled, drawing him down to her again.

"Our family will be strong survivors," he whispered against her cheek.

"Do you think so?" she asked sleepily.

"How could they not be?" North asked, "when you're the mother of them all?"

* * * * *

Be sure to look for
COLORADO COURTSHIP
by Carolyn Davidson.

The next exciting book in the
COLORADO CONFIDENTIAL
miniseries! Available in February 2004
from Harlequin Historicals. Turn the
page for a sneak preview...

Prologue

Saint Louis—April, 1862

He wanted her.

With but a single glance he acknowledged the desire flaring within him, knew instinctively she would fit neatly into his arms should he lift her against himself. His mouth tightened, as did the pressure of his knees against the sides of the horse he rode, and the black gelding sidestepped, tossing his head impatiently.

Appearing small and fragile beside the tall wagon, the woman's face was in profile, her features finely drawn. Woman? She seemed but a girl, clad in a poorly fitting, voluminous dress. From beneath her sunbonnet, dark hair hung in a long braid down her back, the end tied with a bit of ribbon. It was a feminine touch, almost an aching reminder to the watching eye that, no matter the adversity, a woman's need for such small fripperies would prevail.

To Finley Carson's narrowed gaze, she appeared too delicate for the rigors of traveling across prairies toward the mountains that beckoned the unwary. Silently, she stood looking upward at the seat, and then placed a slender hand on the wooden vehicle, hesitant, obviously fearful of climbing upward, lest she fall.

"Get in, Jessica." The order was growled impatiently, the man standing beside the pair of oxen apparently not given to gallantry. Harsh syllables that offered no leniency to her smaller stature, her obvious fear.

"I'm not sure I can," she answered "There's nothing for me to step up on." Her voice was husky, that of a woman full-grown, but laced now with frustration only too clear to a bystander.

And a bystander was exactly what he must be, Finley Carson reminded himself. No matter that the man muttered an obscenity as he stalked back to where the woman stood, it was not *his* concern that she was lifted and tossed with careless movements to sit atop the seat. Not his affair to wonder at her rough treatment by the man whose actions brought quick tears to her eyes and caused her to cringe from his uncaring hands.

Yet, the aching awareness of dark hair and fragile-boned femininity made Finn frown. The urge to rest callused palms upon her narrow shoulders, to look into those wary eyes, tugged at him. For a single moment he knew envy of another man, such as had never possessed him in his twenty-six years.

His hands tightened on the reins of his mount and moved with an almost unseen signal, turning his horse aside. The black gelding obeyed with a toss of his head, and Finn caught a glimpse of the woman's face as she turned her head in his direction. Unsmiling, she nodded, a simple acknowledgement of his presence, and he felt a lurch in his chest as controlled anger gripped him.

He wanted her. Ached to lift her from where she huddled on the high seat. Yearned for a long moment to feel her softness against his body. The thought possessed him and he turned aside, his heels again nudging the barrel of his mount, urging him into an easy lope.

With a discipline gained form his years as an army scout, Finn Carson put the dark-eyed female from his mind, his jaw firm as he rode down the line. of wagons. His gaze surveyed the men who performed last-minute chores, readying the train for its imminent departure from Saint Louis, heading for Independence, Missouri.

This was an assignment he almost relished, one that must be uppermost in his mind over the next months. Taking his place on this wagon train as a guide, using his skills to find the man who was a cheat—a murderer who had stolen the deed to a homestead. One hundred and sixty acres of land that lay in the shadow of Pike's Peak—a speck of wilderness that held a fortune in gold in its depths, if the assayer's office could be relied upon.

Lyle Beaumont. The man was here, his presence a canker, his very existence a stain on the essence of decency Finn had been raised to believe in. Lyle Beaumont—the man who had cheated Finn's brother, Aaron Carson, of his rightful claim to land and then killed him to conceal the theft.

Lyle Beaumont—who even now possessed the deed to those 160 acres in Colorado.

It was toward that man his mind must focus, that man Finn must identify and pursue, even as he hid his own identity on this train. With regret, he set aside the moment of yearning he'd suffered, acknowledging his purpose would not—could not—include a dalliance of any sort on this journey. Certainly not with a woman who so obviously was already possessed by a husband.

There were only a dozen or so females counted among the group. Most of the men were miners who traveled toward the promised land of gold and silver that courted their interest. More of an obsession, actually, Finn decided with a shake of his head. Men who lusted after gold were a breed apart. Willing to sacrifice everything they possessed on the altar of greed.

Even a woman—a woman obliged to follow the path her husband took. A woman who was off-limits to other men, he reminded himself. A woman bound to the man who had placed a ring on her finger and fear in her heart.

HEAD FOR THE ROCKIES WITH

Harlequin Historicals®
Historical Romantic Adventure!

AND SEE HOW IT ALL BEGAN!

Check out these three historicals
connected to the bestselling Intrigue series

CHEYENNE WIFE
by Judith Stacy
January 2004

COLORADO COURTSHIP
by Carolyn Davidson
February 2004

ROCKY MOUNTAIN MARRIAGE
by Debra Lee Brown
March 2004

Available at your favorite retail outlet.

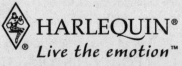

HARLEQUIN®
Live the emotion™

Visit us at www.eHarlequin.com

HHC0

PICK UP THESE HARLEQUIN HISTORICALS AND IMMERSE YOURSELF IN THRILLING AND EMOTIONAL LOVE STORIES SET IN THE AMERICAN FRONTIER

On sale January 2004

CHEYENNE WIFE by Judith Stacy
(Colorado, 1844)

Will opposites attract when a handsome
half-Cheyenne horse trader comes to the rescue
of a proper young lady from back east?

WHIRLWIND BRIDE by Debra Cowan
(Texas, 1883)

A widowed rancher unexpectedly falls in love with
a beautiful and pregnant young woman.

On sale February 2004

COLORADO COURTSHIP by Carolyn Davidson
(Colorado, 1862)

A young widow finds a father for her unborn child—
and a man for her heart—in a loving wagon train scout.

THE LIGHTKEEPER'S WOMAN by Mary Burton
(North Carolina, 1879)

When an heiress reunites with her former fiancée,
will they rekindle their romance or say goodbye
once and for all?

Visit us at www.eHarlequin.com

HARLEQUIN HISTORICALS®

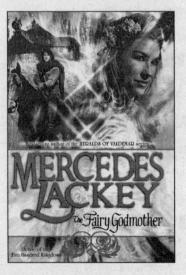

TAKE A TRIP TO THE OLD WEST
WITH FOUR HANDSOME HEROES
FROM HARLEQUIN HISTORICALS

On sale March 2004

ROCKY MOUNTAIN MARRIAGE
by Debra Lee Brown

Chance Wellesley
Rogue and gambler

MAGGIE AND THE LAW
by Judith Stacy

Spence Harding
Town sheriff

On sale April 2004

THE MARRIAGE AGREEMENT
by Carolyn Davidson

Gage Morgan
Undercover government agent

BELOVED ENEMY
by Mary Schaller

Major Robert Montgomery
U.S. Army major, spy

Visit us at www.eHarlequin.com

HARLEQUIN HISTORICALS®